By the same author

Boss of the Pool
Games . . .
Hating Alison Ashley
Halfway Across the Galaxy

People Might Hear You

Robin Klein

Viking Kestrel

VIKING KESTREL

Penguin Books Ltd, Harmondsworth, Middlesex, England
Viking Penguin Inc., 40 West 23rd Street, New York, New York 10010, U.S.A.
Penguin Books Australia Ltd, Ringwood, Victoria, Australia
Penguin Books Canada Ltd, 2801 John Street, Markham, Ontario, Canada L3R 1B4
Penguin Books (N.Z.) Ltd, 182–190 Wairau Road, Auckland 10, New Zealand

First published by Penguin Books Australia 1983
First published in hardback by Viking Kestrel 1987
Copyright (ᶜ Robin Klein, 1983

Typeset in Palatino

Printed in Great Britain by
Richard Clay Ltd, Bungay, Suffolk

For Mary Cleaver McMaugh

One

It was while they were living in the tiny flat above the take-away food shop that Aunt Loris began to change. Frances, preoccupied with the problem of having started at a new school half-way through a term, noticed her aunt's strangeness, but didn't worry about it very much. Aunt Loris quite often was discontented. Frances was skilled at gauging her uncertain moods before asking for things.

She waited until a whole week had passed and Aunt Loris still hadn't done anything about visiting the laundromat. 'I've got no clean jeans left, Aunty,' she said diffidently. 'I tried to dry some in front of that little radiator, but it didn't work too well.'

Her aunt was getting ready to go out. She didn't change from the skirt and pullover worn to work that day. She tidied her long hair at the mirror, not really seeing her reflection, but gazing through it with such introspection that she wasn't really aware of Frances, either.

'And there's not one tea-towel fit to be used,'

said Frances, coasting from diffidence to mild indignation. 'No tea-towels is a health hazard. I could take all that stuff down to the laundromat if you give me some money, and I'd come straight home and not hang round the milk bar. I wouldn't stay downstairs talking to Mrs Wallace, either. I don't want to wear school uniform tomorrow. Our form's going on that excursion, and the other kids will be wearing jeans.'

'No lipstick,' she thought, watching her aunt. 'What's got into her? She ought to wear lipstick. Looks old like that, without it. Plain.'

Aunt Loris knotted a scarf around her hair and slipped on a raincoat, checking her handbag to make sure of the keys. 'Don't open the front door to anyone while I'm out,' she said automatically, as though Frances, too, were just another item to be checked. 'I can't say when I'll be in, but I don't want to find you still up watching rubbish on television when I get back. And just don't let me catch you hanging around that lady downstairs. She's got that food shop to run. And no, you can't go down Scully Road by yourself this time of night.'

'Then I'll just have to have a shot at washing my windcheater in the sink and trying the radiator again,' Frances said. 'Why don't we get a clothes dryer on hire purchase?'

Aunt Loris glanced round the cramped living-room with its couch that became a bed for Frances at night, and the table that held a permanent assortment of dishes and utensils because there wasn't enough cupboard space. 'There's no use complaining and carrying on, Frances,' she said. 'Just be thankful you have a roof over your head and no worry about where your next meal's coming from. I do my best, and I certainly didn't ask to get landed with a kid not even my own to bring up. And where'd you get that hire purchase idea from? You can forget about that. You're picking up a lot of ideas I don't care for at that school. Hire purchase, and can you buy clothes on the lay-by, and can you get your lunch at the tuckshop like the other kids . . .'

'I only asked you once. And I haven't had any new jeans for ages.'

'There's no point nagging about new jeans, because I'm not interested. You'd look much better in a skirt or a dress, anyhow.'

Aunt Loris opened the door onto the metal staircase which spiralled down into the back yard belonging to the shop. Wind curled in through the door while she struggled with an umbrella and negotiated the steep, wet steps. Frances closed the door after her, shoving out the wind. She felt annoyed and cheated. She looked forward to laundry nights and the cheerful laundromat in Scully Road with its piles of magazines, and waiting, lazy customers who sometimes gave her ten cent tips to run down to the milk bar and buy them cigarettes.

'Going out just about every night now,' she grumbled to herself. 'Bet she's got a boyfriend.

Some boyfriend! Doesn't even bother to come and pick her up when it's all cold and wet like this!'

She hitched up the blind and watched her aunt walking downhill to the station, huddling under the umbrella as though to shelter from people as well as rain. She crossed over at the corner, forgetful of traffic, and Frances imagined the shriek of brakes on the wet road. She recommenced breathing as she saw the umbrella, still upright, safe on the far pavement.

'Strewth!' she thought. 'Goes round in a dream half the time, she's getting that dithery. She needs a whole troop of boy scouts to take her over the streets.'

She let the blind drop and hunted for something to wear to the school excursion. The laundry was a messy, unlovely tangle in a plastic basket and her spare jeans and windcheater were at the bottom. She realized that there was no hope whatever of getting them washed and dried overnight. The jeans she wore would have to do, with some primitive homestyle dry cleaning and a long session with the steam iron.

'I'll just have to keep my parka on all day so no one notices my school jumper,' she thought. 'Looks like it'll be cold enough, anyhow. And if I stay with Kerry all the time, she won't let any of the kids get nasty about my clothes.'

Kerry Hodges was one of the reasons why she hoped that this time she could see more than a

4

year out at the same school. Aunt Loris moved restlessly from one job to another, one rented flat to another, and every time they moved, Frances usually had to transfer to another school. She didn't mind the moving into new flats so much. Each time she hoped that they might be going somewhere nicer, and was disappointed. Aunt Loris had no training for any highly paid job, and the flats which she could afford were usually identical – cramped for size, and bearing legacies from the previous tenants, such as scuff marks, loose door handles and ancient newspapers lining all the kitchen shelves.

Ironing her jeans, Frances fantasized about a new life. 'Maybe she's met a rich guy this time,' she thought. 'And as well as rich, he'll be nice, not like those other creeps she's gone out with. And he'll have a fantastic house with a garden, some-where posh, and we'll move in there. And I'll have a proper room, not just the couch shoved up in a corner. Or, if it isn't a guy making her so moody, maybe she's been offered some terrific job. She's just about had that crummy old job at the ware-house. Maybe she's been offered a job as cook on a cattle station, and I could ask Kerry up for the holidays and we'd go horse riding. And if Aunt Loris hasn't been offered a terrific job like that, then perhaps I'll find a new one for her in the paper.'

When she finished ironing, she spread out the newspaper to the situations vacant column. She blew away the pretty bubble castles she'd been making in the air, knowing that it was pointless searching through the well-paid professional columns. Aunt Loris had no skills such as shorthand and typing, or even the ability to work a switchboard. Frances glanced through the factory jobs, no different from the one her aunt had now, and ran her finger down the housekeeper-wanted ones. She skipped those that required a live-in housekeeper. People didn't want full-time housekeepers who had a twelve-year-old niece to support. There were several situations where people needed a housekeeper to live in and some of those jobs sounded really good.

She felt a pang of guilt, as though Aunt Loris were there reading over her shoulder, and silently accusing, Without you I'd be much better off. You're not even my own daughter, but I'm lumbered with you until you're big enough to earn your own keep!

Guilt and loneliness. Frances battled, with a certain courage, the self pity that was beginning to make her eyes sting. 'It's only this gloomy weather,' she told herself briskly. 'Enough to make anyone feel blue. Anyhow, she never really means it when she goes on about being landed with me. She's never dumped me in a home or anything, or run off and left me. It's hard on her, I guess. Women her age, they usually have their own houses, all fixed up nicely, and a husband, and a proper family.'

She looked round the flat, wishing there was some way she could brighten it up a little. It was neat and clean enough, but there was a vast distance between neatness and style, she thought ruefully. You needed money to buy carpets and hanging plants in pots and glamorous wallpaper. And maybe something more was needed, too, and that was actually owning the place where you lived.

'You can't put up posters,' Aunt Loris would say. 'They'll leave marks on the walls and the owner will take it out of the bond money', or 'You needn't put cup-hooks in that door frame, Frances. It's not our flat. Not worth it, anyway, hanging a curtain up there, the lease runs out in June.'

Frances shoved the newspaper aside impatiently. She watched an old film on television, swallowing yawns and boredom, and then had a shower and got into her pyjamas. The sheets on the couch needed a trip to the laundry, and she tried not to think about Kerry Hodges's bedroom, where the bed had drawers underneath and a smart bookcase at the head and lambswool rugs on the floor. She made herself a cup of cocoa and put it on the floor next to the couch while she searched for something to read. Aunt Loris wasn't a reader of books, but sometimes she bought women's magazines on her way home from work.

Frances went into the bedroom to see if she could find one. There weren't any magazines on the bedside table, but its top drawer held a glossily new, zippered briefcase. It was neat and businesslike, and somehow didn't seem to have much in common with her poorly educated and woolly-minded Aunt Loris. Frances, knowing quite well that she shouldn't snoop, opened the zip curiously. The case was filled with typewritten folio sheets, and she took them out to the other room to read in bed while she finished her cocoa.

The pages were clipped together and seemed to be some sort of lecture about religion. Various sentences were underlined and there were explanatory notes added to the margins in large dark handwriting. Frances read bits aloud, making her voice deep and dignified, as though she were a minister preaching a sermon in a television film. 'Only this stuff's more like someone bossing people around,' she thought. 'And telling them a whole bunch of things they aren't allowed to do, or else they'll be struck down dead. And telling it all in a big loud scary yell!'

And the expansive handwriting added to the pages, she decided, looked almost like a yell, too, ordering everyone to take heed or else!

She couldn't understand what it all meant, and put the pages neatly back into the briefcase in the bedside table. She wondered what Aunt Loris was doing with churchy stuff like that. Every time she started at a new school, and brought home the form to be filled in about religious instruction classes, Aunt Loris always wrote down that she didn't want Frances to attend. 'I'm not going to have your head filled up with a lot of nonsense,' she said. 'I don't hold with any of those churches. They're all like old machinery, worn out and useless and run down. If I wanted you brought up in a religion, it would have to be something I believed in all the time, not just for Christmas and weddings and that. Something that really convinces me. I haven't found it yet, that's for sure, though I've been looking all my life.'

Frances cleaned her teeth and slipped the safety chain from the door so that her aunt could get in when she came back. She wasn't nervous on her own. She pulled up the blind and watched the lights dancing in the rain. That was one nice thing about this flat, they were upstairs and had a wonderful view of the suburbs in a night-time splendour of diamonds. The diamonds were clustered thickly where the city lay, and dwindled to a sprinkling where the suburbs merged into the soft, dark hills.

Water chattered on the metal awning of the shop below her window, and turned Scully Road into a silver ribbon. She fixed the pillows so that she could fall asleep watching the vast spread of lights, and the immense, clean sky filled with rain.

Two

Two months went by before Aunt Loris told her
what was happening. 'I want you to give this note
to the headmaster,' she said on the last day of the
school term.

'What's it about? I said I didn't mind missing
out on the summer camp. I know you can't afford
it now you've left your job.' Frances waited hopefully, wondering if Aunt Loris would explain
about that. Four weeks back she'd said casually,
'No need to set the alarm clock on early for me.
I don't have to get up for work. I've left the warehouse. I'm busy doing something else for a bit.
Sort of studying.' She still went out during the
days and quite often at night, and when she was
home, she shut the door of her bedroom and
Frances could hear the rustle of pages being
turned for hours on end. Frances accepted the
new routine and even boasted jauntily to Kerry at
school. 'Aunt Loris is studying,' she said. 'It's
something really hard and important. History and
religion or something.'

10

Aunt Loris sealed the note to the school in an envelope and didn't meet Frances's eyes. 'I wasn't planning to tell you until you got home this afternoon,' she said awkwardly. 'You won't be going back to that school next term. We're moving. That's what I was going to tell you.'

'I'll have to ask them for a school transfer notice, then,' Frances said, keeping her face, from habit, masked with unconcern, so that no one could possibly guess how unhappy she was. 'Kerry,' she was thinking, with a wrench at her heart. 'The first kid I ever met at any school who asked me to be her best friend. The only time I was ever in a place long enough to make a best friend. And she never minded that I didn't have nice clothes or a posh home. Never even noticed. We just liked each other straight off.'

'There's no need to wait around for a transfer notice, Frances. It's likely there'll be a change in your education, anyhow, some other arrangement. I've come to realize that those schools you've been going to are all wrong. It's my fault, for not seeing the bad influences sooner. Lucky you're still a child and things can be changed.'

Frances felt the wrench again, harder to ignore. Cheerless and difficult it might be, living in poky little flats with Aunt Loris and coping with her restless unhappiness, but at least she belonged somewhere. 'You're not . . .' she began, and stopped, battling hard to keep the mask from slipping.

'What?'

'Going to put me in a kid's home, are you?' Frances blurted. Sometimes, when her aunt had had a particularly trying day at her job, and bills had arrived, she often had insinuated that. But she would look ashamed afterwards and, although she never apologized, she would make something nice for supper to show that it had just been tiredness and worry speaking.

'I wouldn't put you in one of those places,' Aunt Loris said. 'The same bad influences would be there. Anyhow, you're my sister's girl, and I have a duty to raise you properly. And that's something I haven't been doing too well up to now.'

'We've been getting along okay, haven't we?' Frances said, puzzled, for it was obvious that Aunt Loris had something more to say, and was having difficulty.

'The reason we're moving, Frances, and why I've given up my job at the warehouse is that I'm going to be married,' she said at last. 'And the wedding's at ten thirty this morning.'

Frances would have rushed to hug her, if she hadn't been wary from experience, knowing that Aunt Loris wasn't the sort of person who gave or received hugs. 'Can I tell the kids at school?' she asked, when she found her voice, lost in a surge of wild joy. 'Can I tell Mrs Wallace?'

'I don't want you spreading it around at school or anywhere else,' said Aunt Loris. 'I don't want people knowing our business. It's going to be a

12

very quiet wedding. This morning at the ceremony, there'll only be myself and Finley, that's the name of the man I'm going to marry, Finley Tyrell. And straight after the wedding, I'll be coming back to the flat to get it cleaned up and everything packed. Some time tonight we'll be moving over to Finley's house. We aren't going away anywhere for a holiday, because he's a widower. He's got a family to look after, same as I've got you.'

'Where did you meet him, Aunty Loris?'

'Through my job at the warehouse. He came in one day to buy some rolls of curtain material and I handled the order. While he was waiting, we just got talking. Or rather, I got talking. I was feeling sort of low that day. Lonely. He seemed really kind and sympathetic when I happened to mention you, and understood how tough it was bringing up a kid all alone. He certainly didn't need telling about that, I realize now, with three girls of his own and his wife dead. I knew he was different, right from the start. Not a bit like those others.'

Frances was silent, remembering several ill-considered relationships which her aunt, from loneliness, had initiated. All of them had ended in bitterness and hurt.

'Finley's so different from all those others. I just can't get over it, me with not much of an education, and a man like that could look at me twice, let alone ask me to marry him. I never dreamed anything like this could happen to me. You'll see, our life's going to be much better from now on.'

'I'm coming this morning, aren't I, to see you get married?'

'I already told you, there's only going to be me and Finley. And the people who supervise things in Finley's church. And that's another thing, it's not like the churches you know about. It's quite different. We call it a temple. That's what I've been studying these past few weeks, about the religion of the temple. When I got to know him better, he told me about the temple. Not all at once, just leading up to it. And I realized it's what I've been searching for all my life. Something that makes sense out of the whole mess. It's an honour, there's no other word for it, that they've decided I'm the right sort of person to belong to it. They don't let just anyone in. But Finley could see that I was willing to study and learn and make a commitment. It's been decided that I've learned enough now to belong and I'm ready.'

'Why won't they let me go to my own aunty's wedding? And his kids, won't they be there? They'd want to see their Dad getting married again.'

'Children don't attend weddings there. We don't believe in it. What I want you to do is take that note to school, and you're not to blab about me getting married, or us moving, not to the kids at school or that woman in the shop. Not on any account. I already told her last night we're moving, and it's none of her business where or why. Rent's been paid up in full, and all the bills settled. And when you get back this afternoon, if I'm not here, you can start in on the packing and cleaning.'

'Do I have to go to school? I want to stay here and help you get dressed up nicely. And your hair, haven't you got time to nip down the street and have it set? If you told them it was for a wedding, they'd fit you in. And flowers, we've got to have a bunch of flowers for you to carry —'

'All that sort of thing's unnecessary. You think too much about clothes. Finley's girls don't carry on like you. You're going to have to be on your best behaviour, Frances, and not let me down. One of his girls is your age, and the other two a bit older, but they aren't like those rough kids you know at high school.'

'Kerry's not rough,' Frances protested. 'You said you liked her, that time she came over here to visit. Can I invite her to the new house in the holidays?'

'It's a fair way from here,' Aunt Loris said evasively. 'And I doubt that you'll need Kerry or anyone else, now you'll have Finley's daughters. You'll have cousins now, only I suppose they'll be more like sisters than cousins, all living in the same house. And it's a lovely big house. You've never lived in a proper house before. We'll both be very happy and safe there.'

'Safe from what?' Frances wondered.

'Get off to school now. You don't want to make me late for my own wedding, do you?' said Aunt Loris. For a moment her face was lit with the happiness that Frances expected in a bride, and forgetting about being wary she gave her aunt a hug.

She went to school, but only for long enough to give the note to the Principal's secretary. 'It's from home, and I don't have to wait for an answer,' she said, breathless from running two blocks.

'You're late,' Mrs Cooper said disapprovingly. 'Even if it is the last day, you shouldn't be turning up at school any old time. Holidays start tomorrow, not this morning.'

'There's a wedding on in our family. I only came to bring that note and get my stuff from the locker. Then I'm going to that wedding. I've got special permission,' Frances lied.

While she collected her gym skirt and books from the locker, Kerry, first seat in the row by the corridor windows, looked out at her questioningly. Frances mimed putting a phone to her ear and dialling. 'A big house,' she thought. 'He's sure to have the phone on. We never had a phone, anywhere we lived before. It's going to be great. I can ring Kerry up every night and talk. And even if that house is a long way from here, Scully Station connects with about a million other trains and trams and buses. We'll never stop being best friends, Kerry and me.'

There was no time to wait for morning recess

to explain things to Kerry. Frances hurried out of school and back to the flat, but didn't go upstairs in case Aunt Loris sent her right back to school again. She hid behind the stacked crates belonging to the shop, and waited for her aunt to come down. A wedding was a wedding, she thought stubbornly, and even if they did have that peculiar rule about no kids being in their old church, or temple or whatever they chose to call it, no one was going to stop her being outside when the ceremony ended and giving her aunt a bunch of flowers. She didn't know where she was going to find any, but Aunt Loris was certainly going to have flowers on her wedding day. She didn't have money for train fares, either, but there were various ways of dealing with that; she knew some of them from hanging around the railway station and watching older teenagers.

When Aunt Loris came down the staircase into the yard, Frances peeped out between the crates and was disappointed at her appearance. She'd thought that her aunt would somehow look different and elegant, going to her wedding, in spite of her talk about clothes. She hadn't done anything special to her hair; it was just pulled back and tucked under a black woollen cap. And she wore the same dowdy suit that she'd bought three winters ago. Nobody gave her a second glance as she walked down Scully Road. In the Friday-morning shopping crowd she was practically unnoticeable; a plain woman in her forties with a reserved manner, and a face that held nothing more remarkable than patience. She bought a ticket at the railway station and went into the waiting bay. Frances strolled casually past the ticket office and went to the opposite end of the platform.

There was a shrub starred with creamy flowers growing behind the platform fence. Frances reached through and broke some off, gathering them into a posy. Those would do as a start, and she would pick some more at the temple. Something as grand as a temple would surely be set in a magnificent garden.

A city-bound train came, and she was able to sneak into the other end of the same carriage that her aunt chose. The train travelled all the way into town, but Aunt Loris remained seated even when they reached the main city station. Passengers left in a great surge, leaving the carriage almost empty, and Frances had to slide to an almost horizontal position in her seat.

The train went through suburbs on the other side of the city. Frances had never been as far as that, and would have liked to look out the windows at the river opening into the harbour and the dockyards and all the places they passed which were completely unknown to her.

At last the train stopped at a station called Bowan, and Aunt Loris got out. Frances left by the other door and slipped into the waiting room, trying to look as casual and innocent as the teenagers she'd seen train hopping from Scully Road. Aunt Loris was the last person to go through the ticket barrier. Frances, watching, reflected that she always did that, always stood back humbly in queues as though she didn't have the same privileges as other people.

When the attendant went back into the office, Frances sauntered inconspicuously through the gate and down the ramp after her aunt. And then she ran. Aunt Loris was walking quickly down the street, a fair way ahead. Frances hurried to keep her in sight, ready to jump into the nearest driveway if she turned around. Even though the whole business was nerve wracking, she began to feel happy and excited as well. A temple, when she thought about it, sounded more picturesque than a church. She imagined it as having white marble pillars and lawns as velvety as carpets.

She decided that perhaps she'd better not help herself to any flowers in the temple garden, and as she trailed her aunt, she inspected front yards in the hope of adding to the surprise bouquet.

Very few of the houses in that street, however, had flowery gardens. The houses were small and shabbily old, built close to the street, and mingled with them were development sites and empty buildings with boarded windows. It seemed a sad, grey place, and it became increasingly difficult to imagine a temple with marble pillars in the middle of such a derelict suburb.

Aunt Loris turned up a side street and halted

at a gateway set in a high brick wall. She rang a bell and waited nervously, fidgeting with her collar. One hand stole up to smooth her hair. Watching from the corner, Frances found something infinitely touching about the gesture, and suddenly wanted to run forward and throw her arms around Aunt Loris and say, 'Don't get married like this! It's not right, being married with no one making a big fuss about you!'

Someone opened the gate and her aunt stepped inside. Frances came out of hiding and went to investigate, but the gate was locked and the wall too high to climb. She was determined to find a way in. Even if she hadn't been invited to the wedding, she was still going to see what the temple looked like. She thought of ringing the bell, which would have ensured at least a quick glimpse of the marble pillars, but she didn't know who was in charge of opening the gate. What if it were Mr Tyrell, and that was his first impression of her, a nosey little stickybeak?

On one side there was a cottage barely visible behind a jungle of tangled rhododendron bushes. Frances scrambled through them to the fence separating the house from the temple property. A long snarl of flesh rippled up one shin, and a branch snapped painfully into her face. She swore softly and hoisted herself above the bushes and onto the dividing fence. She took one long, incredulous look.

'So what was I expecting?' she thought harshly.

'The Taj Mahal? Garn, how dumb can anyone get!' Disappointment drove ugly lines across her forehead.

The temple was a building made from grey concrete slabs, unattractive and intimidating. Heavy metal screens meshed the windows facing the street. The area between fence and building was paved with pebbled concrete, and the only garden was a fringe of thick, fleshy grass blades which had crept up all around the foundations. The building looked like a great toad squatting in a clump of weeds.

'Fancy choosing a place like that to get married in!' Frances thought scornfully. 'Some wedding!' She scrambled down from the fence and back through the bushes to the street, not bothering to wait around with the gift of flowers. They couldn't be reconciled with that grim building behind its locked gate. She threw the bouquet into a bin in front of a service station, and marched, belligerent with disappointment, back to the railway station.

It started to rain, smearing the caked dust on the train windows to an ochre-coloured web. 'I should have stayed at school and spent the last day with Kerry,' she thought dismally. She wished that she hadn't taken it into her head to follow her aunt to the wedding; it would have been more pleasant to live with her dream of a temple with fluted columns and green lawns. Everything about that other place depressed her.

And most depressing of all was that when Aunt Loris did get a chance to marry, it had to be somewhere awful like that. And wearing a three-year-old suit, as though the grey sullen day was no different from any other day in the whole weary year.

Three

When Frances got back to the flat she started the packing. She brought up some empty cartons from the yard and packed all the groceries, scrubbing down each shelf as she finished. She filled the sink with hot soapy water and put in the iron bits from the top of the stove to soak. They had moved house so many times that she knew exactly what to do and the easiest way to go about it. There wasn't a great deal of heavy cleaning to tackle. Aunt Loris had always had a mania for cleanliness and order, in spite of her recent vagueness.

When the kitchen cupboards were cleared, Frances began on her personal belongings. She chose a strong, heavy carton and packed her things with as much care as though they were fine china. Into the carton went her collection of coloured bangles, a tapestry picture of a sailing ship that she'd finish one of these days, the rag clown Aunt Loris had given her on a long ago Christmas, and the lacquered music box Kerry had given her for her birthday. And shoeboxes filled with little things that she didn't exactly treasure, but didn't want to throw out, either, because each one of them was a memento of some incident in her childhood.

She folded the crocheted afghan rug which Mrs Wallace from the shop had made for her and then began to pack her clothes. There weren't many. Now that winter had set in, she'd be needing new jeans. She wondered what would happen about clothes now; perhaps she would inherit all the things those other girls had outgrown. She wished she had something nicer to wear tonight when she had to meet those girls for the first time. Kids, she knew from past experience, could be mean about shabby-looking clothes. Aunt Loris had scarcely told her anything about the Tyrell girls. She hadn't told her anything very much about her new husband, either. Frances's ... what? Uncle? Uncle-in-law? Uncle Finley. She tried out the sound of it a few times. She didn't know anything about him at all, except that he belonged to that temple and had made Aunt Loris do a lot of studying before she was allowed to join. And that he hadn't wanted her to get all dressed up smartly for their wedding. Or sent her any flowers.

Frances's face sobered. She put the last of her belongings in the carton and sat still, looking around at the flat. Other times in the past when they'd shifted, she'd been excited and impatient to go, hanging out the windows to see if the taxi truck had arrived yet. Now, suddenly, the flat above the shop seemed a safe little nest, and their upheaval alarming. She had never in her life lived with more than one other person – Aunt Loris.

Maybe the Tyrells wouldn't be all that enthralled about having a new cousin, or sister, or whatever relation she was going to be, especially one with red hair. It wasn't even straight hair, but grew in a wild tangle of curls. You got stirred a lot if you had red hair. People felt free to make unfunny jokes about carrots and sunsets. And if you weren't pretty, you usually made up for it by being brainy, or good at sports, and she wasn't either of those things. 'They'll think they're getting landed with a lemon,' she thought desolately.

When Aunt Loris returned late in the afternoon, bringing food she'd bought from the downstairs shop, Frances looked at it and her stomach felt like a spin dryer. 'You'll have to eat something,' said her aunt. 'We've still got a lot of tidying up and packing to get through, and the truck's coming at six for the furniture. I can't be making a cup of tea or anything once the stuff's all been taken away. Finley can't pick us up until very late this evening. And after that it's a long drive to their house. You can't go all that time without eating.' She chivvied Frances into eating some of the chicken and coleslaw salad. It was an awkward, uncomfortable meal. Frances wanted very much to say something about the wedding, to wish her aunt happiness, but felt too bashful. Aunt Loris didn't look any different; if anything, she seemed more preoccupied, and didn't mention the wedding at all. Aunt Loris finished her meal quickly and began packing. As she finished filling each cardboard box, she put it with the others by the front door. It didn't take long to pack their household belongings, and looking at them, collected in a pile, Frances felt saddened.

It was such a small pile to show for the long years that her aunt had been working. It really wasn't fair. Other people had houses crammed with enviable things, such as stereo sets and beautiful furniture and ornaments. She wished that she could afford to buy an expensive wedding present to make up to Aunt Loris for all those years of doing without. There was a crate of refundable bottles in the yard, she remembered. She could return them to the milk bar and buy something at the little gift shop down near the station. Even a pretty candle would be better than nothing. And on the way, she could slip in and say goodbye to Mrs Wallace. It seemed terrible to leave without saying goodbye.

'Where are you going?' Aunt Loris asked sharply as she headed for the door.

'Just down to tell the food-shop lady goodbye,' said Frances.

'NO!' said Aunt Loris and grabbed her arm and pulled her back inside the flat. 'That woman hasn't got anything to do with us now. Anyhow, it's dark. I don't want you going off outside by

yourself. All those peculiar kids who hang round
Scully Road, it's not safe.'

'But before you never . . .'

'And you've got to have a shower and wash
your hair. When you've done that you'll find a
plastic bag on my bed. There's some new clothes
in it. It'll be very late when we get to the house
and the girls will most likely be asleep, but I want
you to look tidy when you meet Finley for the first
time. I don't want you making a bad impression.'

New clothes! Frances tore into the bathroom
and ripped off her school uniform and dived into
the shower. She shampooed her hair vigorously,
even though she knew it would dry into a hateful
frizz. But she wanted to please Aunt Loris, who
had somehow managed to buy her new clothes,
when she'd had to attend her own wedding looking so plain and shabby.

She wrapped a towel around her damp hair and
ran into the bedroom to get dressed. A shake of
the plastic bag sent the new clothes spilling across
the bed, and Frances stared at them, aching with
disappointment. Slowly she picked up each gar-
ment and inspected it.

Aunt Loris had bought her a dark wool dress
with a round collar and wrist-length sleeves.
Brown ribbed tights and brown lace-up shoes,
like uniform shoes. A thick knitted cardigan of
drab olive, with sleeves she would certainly have
to fold up several times to make fit. Everything
looked brand new, but she couldn't understand

27

why her aunt had chosen such hideous styles and colours.

'Hurry up and get changed, Frances,' Aunt Loris called. 'The truck will be here in a minute to collect the furniture. They'll need to go in there.'

Frances pulled the dress over her head, scowling at her reflection in the mirror. She put on the cardigan, and buttoned it completely to hide the top of the unflattering dress. 'Having to meet a whole bunch of new people dressed like this!' she agonized. 'Looking like I'm Aunt Loris's little old granny! I just don't know what's come over her.'

Aunt Loris didn't seem to think that there was anything wrong with such an outfit. 'You look nice and neat,' she said approvingly, coming to check. 'You'll have to take good care of those clothes, and always hang them up and not just dump them down anywhere. We'll have to do something about your hair, eventually, too. Let it grow long and plait it out of the way, maybe.'

'I'd rather be bald than wear stupid-looking plaits,' Frances said sulkily. 'What shop did you buy these clothes at?'

'I didn't get them at any shop. Rosgrana Tyrell made them. We were talking about your needing winter clothes, and she got them ready. Rosgrana is the eldest girl. She might teach you to sew as nicely as she does. Don't keep shoving your cardigan sleeves up like that, you'll stretch the cuffs.'

'How old is she, that girl with the funny name?'

'Rosgrana's seventeen. And it's very rude to pass remarks about people's names. You're going to have to watch your manners a bit better from now on, Frances.'

Frances said nothing. She watched Aunt Loris shake out her discarded school uniform and pack it tidily with the other clothes in the carton. She wished she was still wearing that instead of the peculiar, old-fashioned things Rosgrana had made.

'There's the removal truck now,' said her aunt. 'They won't want you underfoot. You can go and wipe up the bathroom after your shower, and don't get those good clothes wet.'

Frances kept the bathroom door shut. She didn't want anyone to see her dressed like that, not even removal-van men. After she finished mopping out the wet shower, she sat on the edge of the bath and waited until she heard the men take the last load down the stairs and drive off. Then she came out.

The empty flat looked terribly forlorn and bare. Her aunt's suitcase and the brown briefcase stood in the centre of the living room, and everything else, all their meagre belongings, had been whisked away into the night. 'Why didn't you get them to take along the suitcase at the same time?' Frances asked, puzzled. 'And we should have gone along to the new house in the truck with all our stuff. It would've saved Mr Tyrell, Uncle Finley I mean, the trouble of coming and picking us up.'

'The furniture's not going to the house,' her aunt said, 'there's no need for it there. It's going to be sold to a second-hand dealer. Finley arranged it.'

'I'm not sorry to see the last of my rotten old couch bed, then,' Frances said more cheerfully. 'Aunty, have they got beds at their house with drawers underneath for keeping things in, like Kerry's I told you about?'

'You'll find out when we get there. I want you to sit still somewhere, Frances, and wait quietly. And don't nag at me every five minutes asking what time it is, either. We're going to have a very long wait, and there's no point in your charging about and being restless.' She sat down on the large suitcase, opened the briefcase and began to read intently.

Frances watched her, marvelling that anyone could retire so fast and thoroughly into an inner private world. 'Aunt Loris!' she cried suddenly, remembering. 'The carton with all my things! What if it gets loaded off at that second-hand place with the furniture? All my clothes are in it. What if that carton goes missing?'

'It won't matter very much if it does. Fussing about a couple of pairs of old jeans. It's not really ladylike to wear jeans all the time. Finley's girls never do, and they always look nice. That's how

I want to see you from now on, keeping yourself neat and tidy, and with prettier manners. And stop carrying on about that box, because everything's been taken care of. I'd like some peace after all that work, so you can just stop pestering. Sit down and be quiet.'

'I'm cold,' Frances said balefully, furious about her aunt's lack of interest in the carton's safety, but she had already gone back to her absorbed reading. Frances prowled about the empty flat. She wished she had a biro so she could write her name somewhere for future tenants to know that someone called Frances Parry had once lived there. She'd done that in every flat they'd lived in. If she asked for a pen now, Aunt Loris would want to know why, and Frances was cautious of her new fussy attitudes. Autographing walls, she realized, wouldn't be well received.

The shower screen was laced with a spreading crack. She eased out a sliver of glass and scratched her name and the date on the skirting board, remembering all the other places they'd lived in, all the little rooms with her name and a date inscribed somewhere. 'Other kids collect records and stuffed animals and stamps,' she thought wryly. 'Me, I collect places to live.'

Then she returned to the living-room and the boredom of waiting. She sat on the floor and wrapped the too long dress skirt around her arms and tried to do something about the nervousness that was beginning to swamp her. 'Perhaps they won't like me,' she worried. 'He likes Aunt Loris, or he wouldn't have asked her to marry him, but there's no guarantee he'll like me. And that goes for those three girls. They might be hopping mad he's got married again and to someone who's bringing along a kid they never even met.'

She wished she could stop feeling uneasy, but it seemed impossible to approach Aunt Loris. She was utterly withdrawn into that reading which appeared to bring her so much comfort.

Frances tried to reassure herself. 'That daughter of his with the weird name sent me these clothes,' she told herself firmly. 'She wouldn't have done that if she didn't want me to live with them. Even if they're funny-looking clothes, she still made them specially. I'm being stupid. It's going to be fantastic, having a big house to live in, and a family. Everything's going to be great. Just like it is at Kerry's.'

After what seemed hours of cold and the rain drumming on the roof, they heard the sound of a car in the alley. 'Come on, Frances,' Aunt Loris said. 'We mustn't keep Finley waiting. This is over.' She picked up the suitcase and the brown briefcase, and switched off the light. The door of the flat clicked shut behind them, and Frances followed her down the stairs, not looking back, because she had learned the futility of that years ago. A small van was parked under the street lamp, and a man got out as they approached. Frances made her face convey an impression of the good behaviour that Aunt Loris so much desired. 'This is your Uncle Finley,' her aunt said.

Frances smiled nervously. Mr Tyrell, in his neat suit, seemed incongruous standing in the laneway behind the dilapidated shop. His whole appearance suggested someone who worked in a clean office building, where weather was mastered by air conditioning and plate glass. She couldn't tell what he thought of her. His expression was as smooth and still as milk.

'Hello, Frances,' he said, shaking hands. 'It's very late for you to be up, but it couldn't be helped. You can try to sleep in the back of the van, because we have quite a long drive. Rosgrana put some blankets and a pillow there.'

Frances expected such a solid-looking man to have a large booming voice, but he spoke quite softly. He put the suitcase in the back and helped her in. Then he shut the doors and got in the front seat next to Aunt Loris and they drove away from the flat in Scully Road.

They talked in low voices, not including Frances in the conversation at all. She felt too shy to make any remarks without being invited. There was scarcely any traffic on the roads at such a late hour. They travelled through suburbs, then followed the freeway around the upper edge of the city. It was uncomfortable and jolting, sitting on the floor of the van. She gave up trying to make sense of the unfamiliar, deserted streets and lay down, yawning, with her head on the pillow. It had been an interminable, strange day. She felt exhausted from its events, and the rhythmic swishing of the windscreen wipers lulled her into semi sleep. She dozed fitfully, half listening to the wipers, and the rain, and their two voices, soft as the rain, and when the long drive ended, she had no idea of where they were, or how long it had taken.

A tall fence loomed in the headlights. Mr Tyrell opened a gate taking a long time about it, and drove the van into a yard and under a carport. Aunt Loris leant over and shook her briskly. 'Come on, Frances, quick,' she said. 'I'll get you straight to bed. Be very quiet when we get in the house, and don't wake the others. You'll meet them tomorrow.'

Frances climbed out, light headed with tiredness. Mr Tyrell was shutting the gate. She heard the sound of a metal bar being lowered and the heavy rattle of a chain. 'Come along, Frances,' said her aunt, but at first Frances couldn't see which way to walk in that dark yard. She blinked, and there was the house, like a great black rock against the sky.

'Funny,' she thought sleepily. 'All dark like that. There's no lights in any of the windows. You'd have thought they'd leave a light on to show us the way in.'

Four

She awoke in a dimmed room, knowing that it
was morning only because two panes directly
under the ceiling let in the thin winter sunlight.
The rest of the window was covered with heavy
drapes. She got out of bed and tried to open the
curtains, but they moved jerkily across the rail
and stopped half-way. The tall lower panes were
made of opaque bubbled glass. Frances tugged at
them to let in more light, but they wouldn't
budge. She knotted up the weighty lined curtains,
and turned around to inspect the room. Last night
was a confused memory of dark stairs, being
shushed at every step by Aunt Loris, undressing
by the faint light from the top windows, and
tumbling into an exhausted, dreamless sleep.

The room was spotlessly clean and tidy; even
her clothes were folded neatly over the end of her
bed. Frances couldn't remember leaving them like
that. There was a large double wardrobe and an
extra bed, with a chest of drawers between the
two beds to serve as a table. Frances looked inside

the wardrobe, hoping that while she had slept, her precious carton of belongings had been delivered to the house. But the wardrobe contained only unfamiliar clothes. She took off the long flannelette nightgown which had been spread out waiting for her the night before, and put on yesterday's clothes. She looked at the rumpled bed, wondering if she should make it right away, and if they expected her to get it as perfect as that other one. It was less trouble to leave it unmade and go looking for a bathroom and some breakfast.

Her bedroom, she discovered with delight, was an attic, and there were stairs to reach the bathroom landing below, and more stairs leading down into the rest of the house. The bathroom was old fashioned, but immaculate. The bath had little iron legs like a lion's paws. There was a noticeable lack of clutter in the room; no paraphernalia of shampoo bottles, talcum powder, or shower caps draped casually over taps. All the towels hung along the rail with their edges at an exact level.

Frances washed her face and combed her hair at the basin mirror. The room was cold. She could feel the chill through the soles of her sensible shoes and brown ribbed tights.

'I'm Claire,' someone said at the door. 'You're sharing my room. You must come down for breakfast now.'

Frances spun round and thought for a moment

that she was still looking at her own reflection, for the girl standing there wore clothes almost identical to her own — a dark dress covered by a cardigan, tights, laced-up shoes. She seemed perfectly at ease in the clothes that were making Frances wriggle with self consciousness. She was slight and frail, with pale skin and long smoky dark hair. Her eyes were a strange, clear green, and they looked closely at Frances, and yet didn't look, skimming away when Frances smiled.

'I couldn't get the windows to open in the bedroom,' Frances said. 'You'll have to show me later how they work.'

'There is special machinery that supplies fresh air to the whole house. The windows aren't meant to be opened.'

'Do you mean air conditioning? But it's so cold, I thought that air conditioning was supposed to . . .'

'You must come down and eat now, because they are all waiting to start.' Claire moved away down the stairs, and Frances followed, wondering how anyone could walk so silently on uncarpeted floors, as though she wore ballet slippers on her feet instead of heavy leather shoes. Her own shoes made a clatter, disturbing the quietness of the house.

'In here,' said Claire. 'This is the kitchen.'

The family sitting around the large table turned to gaze at Frances, and she thought that even if she had been wearing her own familiar, comfortable clothes, she still wouldn't have felt confident anyhow. It was impossible to feel confident when people didn't smile at you.

Aunt Loris was stirring something at the stove. 'Frances,' she said. 'I want you to meet your Uncle Finley's other two girls. Rosgrana, who made you that nice dress, and Helen. But you'll have plenty of opportunity to get acquainted with the girls later. There's a rule here that we don't talk at the table during meals, and that's something you've got to learn straight off.'

Frances wanted to ask why they weren't allowed to talk, but Mr Tyrell bent his head over his clasped hands and said grace, and she was plunged into embarrassment. She didn't know what she should do with her hands, and was too shy to bow her head as the others were doing. She had hardly ever been inside a church, though she knew what grace was. It was thanking God for providing food, but listening to Mr Tyrell, it was almost, she decided, as though he were delivering a forceful lecture about all sorts of topics, right there at the table. The lecture went on, disconcerting and intense, and Frances stopped listening because it made her feel too uncomfortable.

When he finished, Aunt Loris set bowls of porridge on the table. Frances ate hers obediently, although she wasn't used to oatmeal. When Aunt Loris had been working, breakfast was always a scatty meal of cornflakes and toast. She examined the Tyrells with interest. Mr Tyrell, she conceded, wasn't bad looking, if only he'd be less serious and unsmiling. He was again dressed in a suit and tie, as though he had to go to work even though it was Saturday. Frances wondered what he did for a living. Aunt Loris hadn't told her yet. Usually women boasted about what their husbands or boyfriends did. Kerry's mother never stopped. 'Dave's a foreman at that factory,' she'd say. 'He's only been there five years but they made him foreman.' Mr Tyrell certainly didn't look as though he worked in a factory like Kerry's Dad. His hands were well kept, they'd obviously never handled machinery of any sort.

She looked across the table at Rosgrana. The name sounded magical, as if it should belong to someone living in a land where castle moats gleamed in moonlight, but this Rosgrana was plain and apparently ungracious. Frances smiled at her shyly, but Rosgrana didn't smile back. She was a big, strong-looking girl, and her eyes, the same clear green as Claire's, were businesslike and direct. 'She's looking at me as though I'm a germ on a glass slide,' Frances thought indignantly. 'And even if he won't let them talk at the table, there's no reason why they can't smile or look a bit friendly.'

Aunt Loris cleared away the empty porridge bowls and placed boiled eggs and a plate of sliced bread on the table. Frances took a slice, wondering why it wasn't toasted. It wasn't shop bread from a packet; it had a thick hard crust and was brown and full of little seeds and husks. She looked around for honey or jam, but there was none set on the table. She started to ask her aunt for some, and blushed when Mr Tyrell frowned slightly and shook his head. It was obvious that the rule about not talking during meals was a strict one. Each of them was silent, and Rosgrana, without a word, passed her the butter.

Frances ate half the slice and couldn't finish the rest, after such an unaccustomed large breakfast. 'Frances, you mustn't leave any food on your plate at meals,' said Mr Tyrell. 'Finish the bread and don't waste it.' He didn't sound grouchy with her, but his personality was so strong that she didn't care to argue. He didn't even look at her to make sure she was doing as she was told, but seemed to take it for granted that he would be obeyed.

Frances slowly and rebelliously ate the heavy bread. She thought suspiciously that Claire looked smug, and even pleased to see her bossed in front of everyone. She was drawn to the other sister, Helen, who like herself, clearly didn't enjoy sitting still and not talking. Helen fidgeted, and kept glancing at the window, as though she were anxious to get outside and make the most of the sunshine while it lasted. She had an arresting, broad-planed face, and hair the colour of autumn, but the beautiful hair was clipped back from her face with ugly hairpins. Her restlessness infected Frances, who finished the bread and stood up. She thought that she'd go and inspect the garden and find out if there were any exciting shops nearby.

'Frances!' said Aunt Loris sternly. 'You sit right down and wait till everyone else is finished!'

Frances gaped at her. Such niceties had never existed when they lived in the flat. She sat down, feeling conspicuous, as though all the Tyrells were appraising her and thinking she was very bad mannered. She folded her hands in the lap of the scratchy dress and looked around at the kitchen, so she wouldn't have to meet any of the eyes.

The kitchen was tidy, with everything in an ordained place. There were no tea-towels thrown carelessly over dishes drying in the sink, or spill marks on the stove. There were no pictures, just a calendar pinned to the wall, and a clock above the refrigerator. It was a large, bleak room, and Frances hoped that when they'd been living there a little longer, Aunt Loris would smarten it up with bright curtains and a shelf of pot plants, so that it would look cosier.

There was a little shelved room, like an oversized cupboard in one corner. She could hardly wait to phone Kerry and tell her she was living in a house with a pantry and an attic bedroom. No need to be explicit about how drab the house was, what she had seen of it, and how they had a peculiar rule about not talking during meals. She was sure that Aunt Loris would change all that, and then she could invite Kerry over and show off.

She hoped that Mr Tyrell would go off to work when breakfast was over, but he sat there and looked at Frances thoughtfully. His eyes were so direct that she had an uneasy sensation that he might possess powers of ESP and know all the crummy things she'd ever done. Such as the time Kerry's young brother had dared her to take a watering can from a hardware shop and stroll past the checkout with it. She hadn't taken it home, she'd left it just inside the door of the shop, after proving to Kerry's brother that she had the nerve. But she felt as guilty as though she had stolen it, with Mr Tyrell inspecting her like that.

'Frances, you're a fortunate girl to have such a good person as your Aunt Loris to care so much about you,' he said at last. 'Because of her, you're able to join our way of life. It's not possible to explain about our temple and its teachings in a short period. There's a great deal to learn, but we'll help you as much as we can. We have certain rules in this house which must be obeyed at all times. They'll seem strange to you at first, but you'll come to see why they're necessary. They are for the good of us all. And when I think you're ready, I'll arrange for you to receive instruction at the temple.'

'You mean like Sunday School?' Frances asked dubiously.

'No, not like that at all. Our religion is for every day we live, every living moment.'

'She's always been quick with her lessons,' said

Aunt Loris. 'I'm sure she'll pick up the rules in no time. Perhaps you could start her on the reading course right away . . .'

'Perhaps not so soon. She has all those other years to eradicate.'

'I couldn't explain things properly to her out there. It was a better idea, like Rosgrana suggested, to wait till she came to the house.'

'I didn't say that it would be easy,' Rosgrana said. 'It's quite different when an adult enters. There's the motivation then, you see. Not that I shan't do my best to help Frances, of course.'

'It's just a matter of explaining things to her gradually. She's willing, I'll say that for her, and you'll find that she pulls her weight.'

'Still, we mustn't expect everything to go smoothly without any trouble at all. Although she's Claire's age, it's been different for Claire, having all of us to lead her from birth. I hope the council made the right decision.'

'I'm sure they have,' said Aunt Loris. 'I thought, maybe if she helped the girls and watched, and was eased into it gradually . . . and later on today, I'll have a few words with her. I know there'll be difficulties, but if you'll be patient and understanding, I'm sure she won't let anyone down.'

Frances listened to them all discuss her, not understanding any of it, and wondered why her aunt's voice sounded so different, almost pleading, as though she were unsure of her own acceptance in this place.

'The situation was approved by the council,' Mr
Tyrell said. 'Of course it will have good results.
Frances, the most important thing is the necessity
of being very quiet. You must learn that right
from your first day of being here with us. You
mustn't ever raise your voice or call out to any of
the girls from room to room. It's because people
outside might hear you.'

Frances nodded obligingly, relieved that the
strange tide of conversation had finally cast up
something ordinary and familiar. Neighbours and
their complaints; she knew all about that, the
petty bickering witnessed in countless rented
flats, the fuss about radios turned up too loudly,
and visitors' cars in the wrong parking bay. 'All
right, I won't make a noise, Uncle Finley,' she
said, willing to please. 'I can be really quiet when
I want to, you ask Aunty Loris. And thank you
very much for letting me come here to live in this
nice house.'

Her aunt smiled at her approvingly. 'You could
start by helping Claire put away some of the
stores,' she said. 'That way, you'll learn where we
keep everything.'

Claire went into the pantry and pushed at one
of the shelved panels, which swung open. 'Wow!'
thought Frances. 'A secret door!' She scuttled after
Claire and found a short flight of steps behind the
little door, leading down into a cellar. 'Hey, wait!'
she called. 'Why's that door made to look like a

cupboard? Was it like that when your Dad bought this house, or did he fix it up? Hey, Claire, don't go so fast, hang on a minute.' She didn't realize that she was almost yelling with excitement.

Claire frowned over her shoulder. 'Father just told you a few minutes ago about not raising your voice. You must NEVER raise your voice, any-where.'

'Well, what if the neighbours *do* hear?' Frances demanded. 'What's wrong with kids just talking? You must have some crabby old neighbours if they barge in and make a fuss about that! If I was your Dad, I'd tell them to get lost.'

Claire, prim with disapproval, took an apron from a hook and tied it over her dress. 'Father said we had to be patient and explain things to you. If you don't practise being quiet all the time, you're likely to forget when it's important, out-side, or at the temple. He said we had to keep reminding you about it until you've learned. It's a very strict rule, being quiet. We don't make a noise because we can't let people outside know that there are so many children living in this house.'

'Only three. Four, I suppose, now I'm here. But your sisters aren't really kids, they're teenagers. Is your Dad renting this place? Did the lease say no children and no pets or something?'

'Father owns this house. The neighbours might make trouble, that's all. And we're down in this room to work, not chat. You'd better put an apron on, too, to save your dress. Rosgrana's very fussy about clothes being taken care of.'

She switched on an overhead light, and Frances blinked and looked around. The huge cellar was lined with open shelving, and the shelves were crammed with various things, mainly foodstuff in tins and packages. 'Is this a sort of warehouse?' Frances asked. 'Is this what your Dad does, work for a supermarket warehouse?'

'What is a supermarket?' asked Claire.

'You've got to be joking! Are you having me on or something?'

'I don't understand what you mean.' Claire said. 'I've never heard those expressions before. And I don't know what a supermarket is.'

Frances realized suddenly that Claire's speech was remarkably free from slang. She spoke as no other child Frances had ever heard, almost like a very precise adult. There was no light and shade in her voice, and no liveliness. 'You must have been to a supermarket. Everyone has,' said Frances. 'What happens if you run out of something right on tea time? Don't you get sent down to the shops then?'

'We never run short of food. All our food is stored here. Father brings supplies in the van and we label it and use it according to the date on the label. And I'm not allowed to go out anywhere during the day. Only sometimes when we go to meetings at the temple, but we usually drive there when there aren't many people about.'

Frances wondered uncomfortably if Claire were perhaps terribly handicapped in some way, despite her adult-sounding speech. Perhaps her family tried to shield and protect her from crowds. She watched Claire warily. Claire opened a carton of tinned milk and carefully pasted blank labels on each tin. 'You could do this part,' she said. 'Write today's date, just as I've done, and I'll stack the tins on the shelves. It's most important that they're stored in the right sequences. This will get you used to our routine.'

Her speech certainly didn't sound as though she were mentally handicapped, but she was the strangest girl Frances had ever met. Even her attitude to the chore of packing away the food was odd. She was as conscientious as a bank teller balancing the books at the end of a day. Frances worked hard herself, but there were three cartons of tins to be unpacked and stored. The first two cartons contained soup and the last one jars of coffee. 'Can't we finish this off later?' she asked. 'I wanted to go outside and see what the garden's like.'

'We never leave a task half finished,' Claire said reprovingly. 'Especially with the food stockpile. None of us knows for certain when trouble could start. That happened to a temple group in New Zealand. People found out about that family and

47

tried to make them give up the children. They hadn't done anything about security or food and weren't able to lock themselves in until their council could arrange to move them somewhere safe. We could withstand a siege for a very long time here. Father's very efficient about security.'

She was definitely unbalanced, Frances thought. She wondered if Aunt Loris had been told that one of the Tyrell children was like this. Maybe Mr Tyrell had needed someone urgently to look after poor Claire while he was at work, and the other girls at school. And that's why he'd married Aunt Loris. 'And perhaps he hasn't even told her yet,' Frances thought suspiciously. 'In case she said she wouldn't marry him, only now she has, and it's too late. She's stuck with it.'

She fixed a label on the last jar of coffee, but Claire didn't go back upstairs. She walked along the shelves making notes in a little memo book. 'What are you doing that for?' Frances asked.

'I am checking what is in low supply so we can replace it. Rosgrana does it thoroughly every month, but we check when we're down here unpacking new boxes, too. You mustn't distract me. It's important to have everything accurate.'

Frances walked around the cellar. She examined the things on the shelves. There were supplies of canned and dried food that would last any family for a year. And there were other things; seeds in packets, electric light globes, candles, rolls of material and tools, neatly labelled and dated.

'I expect that you'll be given this job now instead of me,' said Claire. 'And I'll be given more time to study.'

Frances walked all around the cellar inspecting the shelves. Shoes, still in their boxes, scissors, biro refills, blankets, writing paper, soap, packets of knitting wool, nails, matches.

'I hope that you'll keep it as tidy as I've done,' Claire said. 'Some of those labels you wrote look very untidy. Is your handwriting always so bad?'

Frances was only half listening. She had discovered that the dates on some of the labelled items went back twenty years.

Five

Frances turned away and hurried up the stairs to the kitchen. She stood still, watching Aunt Loris wash up, until she was sure her voice would come out steadily, and not shrill from uneasiness. Then she strolled across the kitchen and picked up a tea-towel. 'That girl,' she said. 'Claire. I don't reckon she's right in the head. The way she's carrying on down there and talking ... half of what she comes out with doesn't make any sense. And the things they've got down there in that cellar! Aunty, have you ever been down in that place?'

'The store room? Of course I have. I've been to this house a lot over the past few months to meet the girls and get used to the routine before we moved in. I hoped you paid attention and watched how Claire put the things away. It's important, even with tinned food, that it's used by a certain date. Don't you ever let me catch you just grabbing the first thing off the shelves if you're sent down there for supplies.'

'That room's weird. They've got blankets and first-aid things and timber and stuff like that stashed away down there, not just food. And labels dating back years and years. They've been collecting stuff down there all that time! What's it all for?'

'It's all going to be needed one day. It's a sort of preparation.'

'What for?'

'Frances, I just don't know how to tell you all at once. The temple religion's different from the ones you've heard about, and it's a hard one to live by. But it's the only true one, out of all those hundreds of religions in the world. We've got people who can see into the future. Everything that's done in this house is for a reason.'

'But it's creepy storing all those things instead of just shopping every week like ordinary people. And Claire said she'd never been to a supermarket. She acts peculiar.'

'She's just been brought up differently from you, that's all. It was very good of Finley to let you come here to live, Frances. Some people at the temple thought it might be too much of a risk, that you'd maybe disturb the children here.'

'What on earth did they mean? How could I?'

'By not being willing to let us guide you. But that won't happen. You'll come to an understanding, same as me. You mustn't ever give Finley cause to regret that he's taken you into this house. You're safe here from all the bad things that go on outside. We're all safe.'

'Everyone's talking as though I've got to join

that religion,' Frances said sullenly. 'No one has even asked me if I want to or not.'

'You'll want to, when you find out why it's necessary. And it's not a case of "joining", either. It'll come to be your whole life, like it is for me. The best thing for you to do is watch Claire and copy the way she does things. Finley's very proud of her, and rightly so.'

'I don't see why. I was telling you, Aunty Loris, only you didn't take any notice, I think Claire's a bit mental.'

'Rubbish. There's nothing wrong with Claire. She's very intelligent for her age. Brilliant, even.'

'She's weird, you mean. Have I got to hang around with her all the time?'

There was the sound of the little door in the pantry being closed gently. Claire was standing by it, and her face was quite expressionless. Frances didn't know if she'd heard, and felt confused and embarrassed. 'They've all got faces like closed windows,' she thought resentfully. She finished drying the bowls and clattered them into place on the dresser.

'Shush!' said Aunt Loris. 'You've got to do things nice and quietly, like Claire when she shut that door just now.'

'The neighbours couldn't possibly hear me dry the dishes.'

'I don't want you arguing, Frances. Besides, your Uncle Finley does a lot of his work at home.

He uses the front room as his office, and you mustn't disturb him with noise.'

'What sort of work does he do?' Frances asked curiously.

'Accounting, for the temple. He handles the income from a few properties they own. You know what an accountant does.'

'Frances is supposed to help me with the upstairs floors now,' Claire said. 'Rosgrana made a new timetable for the housework, when we knew for certain that you'd be coming. On Saturday mornings Frances and I have to do the floors upstairs, and dust the big room.'

'I'd rather help Aunt Loris down here.'

'But it isn't our turn for kitchen work. Rosgrana went to a great deal of trouble to plan the new timetable and share out the work fairly.'

'I don't see why I can't do the floors later. What does it matter what time they get done? Anyhow, they looked as clean as a whistle this morning.'

'Frances!' Aunt Loris said sternly. 'You're to do as you're told. This house is run in a certain way, and I won't have you questioning it in that insolent manner.'

Claire didn't say anything. She went to a cupboard and got out some cleaning equipment. Frances followed her upstairs, seething. She didn't mind helping, but hated being bossed and organized, in what was supposed to be her school holidays.

Rosgrana sat sewing at a table on the bathroom landing. She was stitching a hem with beautiful, almost invisible tiny stitches, and was so absorbed in the work that she didn't look up as they came up the stairs. Claire filled a bucket with hot water and took it to their shared bedroom. She swept the floor and then mopped it with adult thoroughness. Frances made her bed, still disgruntled, knowing that she'd never get it to look as neat as Claire's, and not trying very hard.

'You shouldn't have knotted the curtains up,' Claire said, untying them. 'Enough light comes in through the top panes. There is no point touching the windows at all. They don't open. Fresh air comes from the machinery Father installed.'

'I'd rather have windows you can open and close than air conditioning. And to see out of, too. That frosted glass is gloomy.'

'The glass is like that to stop people looking in from outside.'

'I wouldn't care if they did,' Frances said cheerfully. 'I'd just wave to them.' She tucked her pillow under the ugly chenille bedspread. 'Hey, I almost forgot,' she said. 'There was a carton that was supposed to be delivered here last night with all my things in it. There's a nice crochet rug someone gave me that could go on this bed.'

'I haven't seen any box,' Claire said. 'And that bed doesn't need any more blankets.'

'I didn't mean it wasn't warm enough. I just want my rug to go on top to make it look pretty.

54

That carton with my stuff in it should have been dropped off here. It had all my clothes in it. I can't wear these I've got on for ever.'

'The clothes in the left-hand side of the wardrobe are yours,' Claire said. 'Rosgrana got them ready. They decided that you needed new things to wear.'

Frances looked more closely at the contents of the wardrobe. The left-hand side held two night-gowns, two pleated skirts, another dress and a couple of shirts and sweaters. There were under-clothes and a knitted wool cap and gloves. She had never in her life received so many new clothes all at the one time, but found no pleasure in them. They were so plain and sombre, and she inspected them uneasily, longing for her own shabby, comfortable things. She couldn't believe that Aunt Loris would have sent her belongings to be disposed of with the furniture.

'Rosgrana worked hard to get those clothes ready,' Claire said. 'Winter clothes are always more trouble to make. I don't think it's very nice of you to look at them like that, as though they're not good enough for you. Not after Rosgrana spent so much time over them.'

'I'm not being ungrateful,' Frances muttered. 'But these clothes your sister made aren't right for doing ordinary things in. Skirts are only for when you go out somewhere special. Soon as my box turns up, I'll get changed into jeans.'

'We received some jeans once, packed by mistake in a warehouse order. Father took them back. He doesn't like to see girls wearing boys' clothes.'

'Jeans aren't just for boys!'

'You're making your voice loud again. I wish you'd remember not to. It's boring, having to tell you all the time.'

Frances knew that she should go and thank Rosgrana for making the clothes, but she was too upset about her missing carton. Perhaps it had been left down in the hall, and she was getting herself into a state about nothing. She went downstairs. The big house was as quiet as a cave. Listening, she could hear vague sounds, her aunt's footsteps in the kitchen, and cooking pots being shifted about; someone coughing; Rosgrana running the sewing machine upstairs; cars passing in the street, but the house seemed to absorb all sounds into its walls and draped windows, so that they were scarcely audible.

The carton wasn't anywhere in the hall. She looked into a large, high-ceilinged room with a central table ringed by chairs with carved backs. There was a glass case containing mounted butterflies and moths, a huge globe of the world on a stand, an open fireplace that had been bricked in to take an oil heater. Dust specks drifted in bars of sunlight struggling through lace curtains at the window. When Frances parted the curtains, she found that the light entered through the slats of wooden shutters protecting the glass on the outside. This window, too, could not be opened.

There were hundreds of books in the room, filling several bookcases, stacked up on the floor, and spread out over the great table. Frances picked up one to read the title. 'You won't understand that,' Claire said from the doorway. 'It's advanced mathematics. And it's not polite, anyhow, to disturb books other people are obviously still using. You mustn't ever touch anyone's books on this table.'

Frances saw a television set at the end of the room, and its presence was like catching a glimpse of a friend in a strange street. She switched it on to see what the reception was like in that area, but no picture appeared.

'Father's adjusted it like that specially,' Claire said. 'There's a part he keeps in his office, and the set can't be used without it. We don't watch ordinary television, anyhow. Father has tapes of films, there's a special name for them . . .'

'Video?' Frances asked hopefully.

'Yes. I was about to say that but you interrupted me.'

'Video! That's fantastic! What films has he got? Can we put on something now?'

'We watch them only on one evening each week. You wouldn't really understand any of them yet. They're used with our temple study programmes.'

'Do you mean they're just documentaries and stuff like that?' Frances asked, disappointed.

'They're supplied by the temple. So they're not

'just' anything. They're very special and important.'

'I'd rather watch ordinary TV,' Frances said. 'There's a show on tonight I don't want to miss. How do I go about fixing up the set so it'll work?'

'You aren't allowed to touch it. Besides, night time is when we study, and we use this room. You'll have to be quiet, then, or you'll disturb us.'

Frances stared at Claire helplessly, overwhelmed by her formidable air. It seemed that every time she made a remark about anything, Claire contrived to put her down. 'I think I'll go outside a bit,' Frances said abruptly.

'I don't want to go outside. But I suppose I shall have to, if you're going.'

'For goodness sake, you don't have to come. I'll have a look around outside by myself.'

'You aren't allowed. There must always be two. And you must ask Father first, or Rosgrana, if he's away. Your aunt doesn't count because she's just new here. Like you.'

Frances marched angrily into the kitchen and confronted Aunt Loris. 'Claire told me I had to ask every time I wanted to go out in the yard,' she said indignantly. 'And you can't turn the telly on. There's something wrong with the knobs, they stick and won't turn around. He has a whole lot of dumb old rules they have to follow, just like a school! Or maybe it's that Claire, her idea of a joke, maybe she's making it all up.'

'Claire wouldn't ever tell lies,' Aunt Loris said.

'And your uncle told you at breakfast that there's rules here.'

'But they're awful, those rules! And Claire's awful, too. She acts as if she doesn't like me coming here to live or touching anything. And that carton with my clothes and things, that truck couldn't have dropped it off here. I want to ring up and find out what they've done with it. I want —'

'Frances there's no use whining to me about every little thing you don't like here. You're going to have to make the best of it. You've got all the clothes you need in that wardrobe upstairs. It's as if someone turned over a book for you to a nice new clean page. That's the way I want you to think of it. You'll be spoiling it all if you come into this kitchen every five minutes with complaints about this that and the other. I've got a lot of work to do.'

Frances hung around, forlorn and hurt. It was clear that Aunt Loris wasn't at all interested in her grievances. She'd settled gratefully into the new house like a ship taking refuge in a harbour.

'Father said you may go outside for a little while,' Claire said severely, coming into the room. 'But you must stay with me all the time. Helen's working in the garden, but she's busy, so I have to be responsible for you. And if you raise your voice and make a noise, you're to come straight back inside.'

She pushed open the kitchen door and a metal

screen door behind it. The screen was set into a heavy frame, and when it swung back into place, it looked as protective as a stout shield. The yard was large, with a vegetable garden and fruit trees, but there was no proper lawn. Most of it was paved with concrete, with a rotary clothes hoist set into the concrete, and the carport and toolshed taking up a great deal of space. It was an extremely tidy yard, but not really any different from dozens of other yards in other suburbs, except for one thing.

This yard was enclosed by a corrugated iron fence topped with strands of barbed wire, and the back gate was fastened with a heavy bar and padlock. The fence was too tall for anyone on the other side to see over, and too high to be climbed from the inside.

Frances walked around the sides of the house to see if the front garden was nicer. But there was no way of getting into it. One side path was blocked with a high brick wall, and the other by a tall gate. Claire watched without comment as she tried unsuccessfully to open the gate. 'Why can't we get through to the front garden?' Frances demanded. 'Why's the back yard all locked up and separate?'

'To keep people out.'

'What about the man who reads the meters? How does he get in?'

'The electricity meters are on the porch by the front door. The gate onto the street isn't locked.

It would call attention to our house, otherwise, if the front looked different from any other house in the street. But we're not allowed to be in the front garden. And there's no reason for anyone not connected with our family to come into our back yard. That is why the side gate is kept locked.'

Frances had to strain to hear Claire, who, since she had come outside, had lowered her voice considerably, so that it was scarcely above a whisper. 'Speak up,' Frances said sourly. 'Honest, Claire, don't you reckon it's overdoing it a bit? As if neighbours would mind a couple of kids talking! It's your own yard, anyhow. You can do what you want in it. Yell at the top of your voice, if you like.'

'You don't understand,' Claire whispered angrily. 'We have to keep quiet to protect ourselves. How can you understand about anything when you have done no study yet? Helen said she was glad that somebody new was coming here to live. I wasn't. I knew it would be tiresome, having to share a room with you, having to show you things . . . Your voice is too loud, and I think we should go back inside the house.'

'I haven't finished looking around yet,' Frances said defiantly. She went to the vegetable garden where Helen was working fertilizer into the soil. Helen wore a denim apron over her clothes, and her hair had come loose and tumbled untidily over her shoulders. She shoved it back and left a smear of dirt across her cheek. Frances decided that she looked much more approachable than either of her sisters. 'I could help you weed,' she offered.

'There's no weeding to be done, because I work out here every day. But when spring comes, you can help me with the planting.' Helen didn't sound particularly gracious, but underneath the surliness Frances sensed a tentative fumble at goodwill.

'I'd like to help,' she said enthusiastically. 'Why don't we grow some flowers? It seems a shame having a yard this big and most of it's concrete. You could get your Dad to build a barbecue and ask your friends around for parties and things. Or a trampoline. Plenty of space here for a trampoline. You can buy them second hand. I knew a kid at school who saved up his paper-round money and . . .'

'Don't talk so loudly!' Claire said. 'I told you not to.'

'So what if I do?' cried Frances, homesick suddenly for the little flat above the shop, where it hadn't been necessary to be quiet, and where you were up high enough to see over the top of any fence. 'So what if the neighbours do hear? I'm not worried.' She felt guiltily pleased at Claire's shocked, indignant face.

'It must be difficult, moving somewhere new to live,' Helen said hesitantly. 'I expect that you feel strange.'

Frances warmed to her sympathy. 'I'll get used to it,' she said. 'Haven't got much choice, have I? I have to go where Aunt Loris goes. And the house is nice, though I'm not used to such a big place. Is that rhubarb, that stuff in a clump there? I hate rhubarb. Aunty Loris used to get it from the market and make custard to go with it, but I still hated it. I hope she doesn't serve it up here.'

'It's sinful to talk about hating good food and not eating what's placed in front of you,' Claire said.

'Everyone has some kind of food they don't fancy,' Frances said exasperated.

'I always eat everything that's put in front of me.'

'I bet you don't eat spinach. Or beetroot. Nobody could eat beetroot.'

'I do. I never waste food.'

'Well, hooray for you, then! And what's more, you can go back inside if you want. I'll stay out here and talk to your big sister.'

'You're supposed to keep with me today, all the time, to learn things. And I won't go back inside just because YOU say so. I'm going in now because I have things to do. And you had better come with me.'

'I'll come when I'm good and ready, and not a minute before!'

'I shall tell your aunt that you don't co-operate,' Claire said, and her footsteps on the concrete sounded as sharp as blows. Frances, however, felt triumphant. She sat down on the wheelbarrow and watched Helen.

'How old are you?' she asked curiously. Although Helen appeared to be in her mid-teens, there was something oddly immature about her. She was nothing like the teenagers at Frances's high school. There was nothing amateurish, though, in the way she set about her work. The autumn crops looked as trim and competent as a garden manual.

'I'm fifteen,' Helen said.

'Wish I was. You can get jobs in the holidays when you're fifteen, and get paid for them!' Frances said. 'If I was fifteen, I'd go fruit picking. You know how kids do, in a group with their friends. Have you ever done that?'

'No, I'd like to, though. Orchards must look beautiful. Father brought a film tape home from the temple once, about fruit growing, and it showed an apple orchard that belonged to the temple. I wouldn't be allowed to work on one. I'm not old enough to leave this house yet.'

'But lots of kids go fruit picking. Sometimes you can go just for the day. If you asked your Dad, maybe I could come along, too. There used to be an apple place that advertised —'

'I told you that I wouldn't be permitted.'

'Well, how about horse riding, then? I'd really like to have a go at that these holidays. There's places you can ring up and book, and they take you out riding in a group for an hour. Want to come?'

'Why don't I do this, why don't I do that!' Helen snapped. 'Chattering on about holidays ... You're being a nuisance, and I'm trying to work.'

Frances got up, jolted by the sudden hostility in her voice.

'Go away,' Helen said, digging the garden fork angrily into the soil. 'You're supposed to be inside helping Claire. Your aunt said that you'd be no trouble and that you'd fit in with us at once. And you'd better. Because otherwise there won't be any room here for you at all.'

Six

Frances was so hungry by evening that the silence at the table didn't seem so oppressive. The meal cooked by her aunt and Rosgrana was lavish. Although it was barely six, it was winter dark outside, but the kitchen was filled with the stored heat from the oven. Frances finished her meal quickly and remembered that she mustn't leave the table before the others.

Everyone in that family, she decided, seemed to be slow and painstaking, as though time in their house moved to different clocks. Frances, used to rushing about from one half-finished task to the next, found their slowness irksome. She made herself sit patiently. There wasn't anywhere she could go, anyhow, except the cold little attic, or the big front room where it wasn't even possible to watch television. And besides, there was a great pile of washing up to be done. She guessed that dirty dishes would never be left lying around overnight in that orderly house.

After the meal, Mr Tyrell and the girls went off

to the sitting room. 'Give me a hand with the drying up, Frances,' Aunt Loris said. 'And get that
look off your face, too. I wanted to talk to you,
and the girls knew it, and that's why they aren't
here helping.'

Frances picked up a tea-towel and wondered
how she could tell her aunt that the Tyrell girls
were treating her badly. She hesitated to spoil
Aunt Loris's obvious pleasure in her new house,
but she wasn't, she decided grimly, going to spend
all the school holidays feeling as though she had
no right to be living there.

'My carton still hasn't turned up,' she said
instead. 'I asked Rosgrana and she hasn't seen it.
She doesn't know anything about it. My jeans,
and that crochet rug, and Kerry's birthday present . . .'

'Finley didn't want you bringing anything like
that here. We agreed it was best to make a new
start and not have anything from before. The carton's with the rest of our old furniture. That's all
done with now. There's no need to look so sulky
about it, either.'

'You could have asked me before you got rid
of all my things!' Frances said bitterly. 'Mrs
Wallace made that rug for me specially. I was
going to keep it as long as I could, to remember
her.'

'We want you to forget everything else and
concentrate on fitting in here. You couldn't do
that with all your old things around. You've got

to do it because of the temple. I told you there's people in it who can see into the future, and what they see is going to be terrible. There'll be a war, a million times worse than the last one, because now they've got all those nuclear weapons. And the only people who are going to come out of that dreadful war alive are the ones belonging to the temple. It's all been foretold.'

Frances concentrated very hard on the plate she was drying. It was an ordinary stoneware plate with a small chip out of the rim. There was something comforting in drying a chipped plate with a blue checked tea-towel; it made the talk of war and destruction seem quite impossible.

'People never want to believe that anything bad can happen to them,' Aunt Loris said. 'It's just greed now, that rules the world. People are only interested in buying new things they don't really need, and leading a bad, sinful life. I was ignorant like that, too, until I met Finley and did all that study and the temple accepted me as a member. And you'll be accepted, too, because you're my responsibility. We're going to live differently now, keeping ourselves on the right path, and we'll have nothing to fear from that war.'

'If those temple people can see into the future, why don't they warn everyone else, so they can be saved, too?' Frances asked.

'Because people wouldn't listen. They're too deep in their sin. That's why, if you're chosen to be a temple member, you have to protect yourself, cut yourself right off so you never get contaminated.'

'But I haven't really been chosen. I only ended up here because you came.'

'Finley's been guided by the temple council. You're still a child, and it's not too late for you to be shown the proper ways. It's difficult, mind you, because you've got to undo all the bad influences from out there. And that's another thing I was going to tell you. We don't ever let people outside the temple pry into our way of doing things. That's why the fence is around the back yard, and why we don't use the front garden, to stop people knowing about us. They wouldn't understand, and they'd try to interfere. People are always scared of what they don't understand. That's why all the temple houses lay up a stock-pile of food and stuff. If we ever had to fight for what we believe in, we'd be able to lock ourselves in and survive for a long time. And in the war, when everything else is in ruins, this house will be spared, because it belongs to the temple and has divine protection. We'll still have food and equipment afterwards to build a new community.'

Frances didn't know whether to feel frightened or sceptical. If she'd heard a stranger, someone she'd just met, coming out with those odd claims, she would have walked away, bored, maybe filled with pity. She would have felt very sceptical indeed. Which perhaps made her, she thought,

69

getting more and more confused, like those other people wallowing in sin and greed who couldn't recognize the truth. But she'd been told all this in this tidy kitchen, by her aunt, who never lied to her, and in the telling Aunt Loris had been speaking in a perfectly matter-of-fact, unemotional voice.

'The people outside would think nothing of coming in here and destroying everything Finley has built up,' said her aunt. 'They'd use force. Jealous, frightened people always use force, it's been the same all through history. That's one of the reasons you've got to be quiet when you're outside in the back yard. All it takes is the wrong sort of person passing on the other side of the fence and hearing, and getting suspicious. You weren't quiet out in the yard this morning, according to Claire.'

'I knew she'd come in and blab,' Frances said resentfully. 'I could just tell by the way she walked, like a policeman.'

'Hush, now. You mustn't talk about anyone in this house like that. It's not like a group of children in school; you've got to be polite all the time and work together. If one person pulls in a different direction the whole set up would be in danger.'

Frances arranged the plates on the dresser. It had carved wood edges and looked cheerful with its rows of cups and graded china. 'It mightn't be so bad,' she thought. 'So what if they all belong to some prissy old church no one ever heard of and they keep going on about a war? I'll follow their rules, because this is their house, not mine. But I won't go to that temple of theirs until I'm sure, and no one's going to make me. Anyhow, school's starting in two weeks. I'll meet a whole lot of new kids there, and I won't have to spend so much time with Claire and those other two. Guess I can stand it.' She smiled at her aunt. 'I won't pull in a different direction,' she said. 'I'll be on my best behaviour, and I won't let Claire get under my skin so much.'

'I knew you wouldn't let me down,' said Aunt Loris, with such obvious relief that Frances had a sudden thought that perhaps her aunt, too, was finding things a bit strange and difficult at this house.

'She's never owned a house before,' thought Frances. 'Now she's suddenly got this big place, and you can tell she's rapt in it, but she's scared, too, with all of them watching to see she doesn't make any mistakes, and that she doesn't pull in a different direction, either.'

'You can go into the front room now,' said her aunt. 'Everyone studies in the evening for a couple of hours and you'll be expected to join in.'

'Can't I stay out here with you?' Frances didn't want to leave the warm kitchen and go into the living-room to be stared at by Mr Tyrell with his alert eyes that could see into the future and maybe into people's past lives as well.

'You have to stick to the timetable, Frances, like everyone else. I'll be in there myself just as soon as I finish tidying up the kitchen.'

Frances went unenthusiastically along the hall and opened the door into the living-room. She was glad to find that the oil heater was switched on, and that the room was warm. Everyone was sitting around the central table with work in front of them. Frances took the chair furthest away from Mr Tyrell. She glanced at the book Claire was reading. It was in a foreign language, but Claire was reading the page rapidly, as though she understood every word. Frances didn't show that she was impressed. Claire finished the page and turned to the next and hesitated at a word. She looked it up in a dictionary and wrote it neatly into a little indexed book.

'Frances, you mustn't sit there and not do anything,' Mr Tyrell said at last. 'This is our study time. You must work at something, too.'

'I haven't got any of my books,' she said. 'They were in the carton with all my other things that didn't arrive.' ('And it's your fault,' she thought. 'You talked Aunt Loris into chucking out all my stuff.')

'We have all the necessary books here. Choose a subject and work at it for this evening.'

'Study? Like Claire's doing?'

'Exactly. I don't mind which book you choose, but you must persevere with it for the rest of the evening. You can't get up and down from the table all the time.'

Frances couldn't think of any subject that she wanted to read about for a whole evening. Claire was looking at her in what seemed to be an unbearably superior manner. 'Handcrafts?' Frances said. 'I like craft at school. We made papier mâché owls last term. And reptiles, we studied them, and the people came to school with all these snakes and lizards and showed us how to milk snake venom and what you do for snake bite. Have you got any books about reptiles? Oh, and when we went down the mine on the excursion, the lady told us about the miners never putting their lunch on the mine floor because of rats. That mine was fantastic.'

'What would you like to study, Frances?' Mr Tyrell asked patiently.

'Rocks and mining,' she said importantly, casting a far superior look at Claire. Mr Tyrell searched through one of the bookcases and gave her a text book called *Basic Geology*. 'Here's some writing paper and a pen,' he said. 'You might find it useful to list all the terms you aren't familiar with.'

Frances opened the book, hoping that Claire was suitably awed by its topic and grandeur. She read all the way down the first page although she couldn't understand very much of it, and self-consciously wrote down a very long list of unfamiliar words. Claire, she thought crossly, would probably be delighted if she had a great long list of things she had to ask about when study time was over. She leafed through the book, pretending to be absorbed in the black-and-white diagrams, but they were just as boring as the text. There was no way she could relate that marvellous descent into a goldmine to the skimpy sketches of rock cross-sections.

Aunt Loris came in and sat down and began to read the papers from her brief case; as though she were studying for some important examination. The silence in the room was as total and oppressive as fog. Frances wasn't used to studying. None of the teachers at the schools she'd attended had ever given out more than a couple of pages of homework to do each night. And despite having to change schools so often, she'd never fallen behind in her work, so hadn't ever had to do extra work on her own to catch up.

'Can I change this book for something else?' she asked. 'This one's got nothing in it about goldmines.' Her voice tumbled like gravel into the fog, and everyone looked up from their work and stared at her. 'Sorry,' she said, abashed. 'I forgot about not talking. I just wanted a proper book, one with stories in it. Science fiction, or something like that.'

'This is our study time, not a time for reading fiction,' Mr Tyrell said.

'But I'm only in form one. They don't expect

you to study in form one. Not in the holidays, anyhow. Claire's only in form one, isn't she, if she's the same age as me? How come they give her all that German or whatever it is at school?'

'We don't go to school,' Claire said.

Frances looked at Aunt Loris and asked bewildered questions with her raised eyebrows. 'That's one of the reasons why you mustn't make a noise outside,' Aunt Loris said. 'There are laws about children having to stay at school till they're fifteen. None of the girls ever went to school. Finley could be taken to court. So we don't want people knowing we've got children and young people living in this house.'

'But everyone goes to school!' Frances said faintly. 'You've got to, to learn and get an education.'

'The girls have been educated at home, not in a school where they'd be exposed to a lot of bad influences. Finley's got books here covering every subject you could think of. Claire can read and write in three different languages, and I bet none of the girls you knew at that high school could do that.'

'They could if they'd lived in a house where you weren't allowed to watch television,' Frances thought scathingly. 'There's just nothing else to do here except read.'

'It's quite easy to study on your own,' Rosgrana said. 'There's no need to look so disbelieving. You could make a list of subjects you don't know very much about, and plan an evening timetable for yourself. Study will become a habit if you approach it in the right way.'

'And once you've settled into the routine, Frances, you mustn't waste time by beginning one subject and stopping after a short time because it seems difficult,' Mr Tyrell said. 'That's not the way we do things here. For a start, I'd like to see you finish that book you have in front of you.'

'But it's too hard. And it's boring. About school, you don't mean that I have to . . .'

Aunt Loris frowned at her across the table. 'That's enough, Frances. The evening are for study. You'll just have to learn to fit in with the rest of us.'

'The rest of us.' Frances stared back at her, appalled. She had a swift, frightening vision of her aunt, with the Tyrell family, on one side of a broad river, and herself abandoned on the other. She tried to concentrate on the geology text. She wished she could sit nearer to the heater, but didn't dare leave the table without asking. And it would be unthinkable to bother Mr Tyrell again. He looked completely unapproachable. He had what Frances took to be a bible in front of him on the table, and was reading intently and making copious notes as though challenging every printed sentence and finding fault with it.

'Not sending them to school!' she thought indignantly. 'Who does he think he is? No wonder Claire's such a pill. He needn't think I'm going to give up school and be stuck in this house with her all day. If he doesn't let me go back to school when the holidays finish, I'll ring up the police and have him arrested for breaking the law.'

Mr Tyrell glanced up from his notes and she hurriedly pretended to be working. She made a list of things she would study in the evenings during the holidays so that she wouldn't be stuck with the tedious geology book again. When she finished, she wondered if she dared pass the list over the table to Rosgrana to find out if they had books on all those subjects. But Rosgrana was studying so hard that she dare not interrupt. Nobody was idle. Helen worked by herself at the far end of the table. She finished reading one book and put it aside, and skimmed through another with restless energy. Her working area was less tidy than the others, with books lying face down to mark pages and a manila folder crammed with disorganized notes.

Claire stopped writing, pointedly, every time Frances fidgeted. Her handwriting was almost as perfect as printed lettering. Frances looked at it and became so ashamed of her own untidy scrawl that she slipped the list into her pocket and decided not to show it to anyone. She tried to read the geology book again, but was so limp from boredom that the letters swam as though she were reading through a slab of flawed glass.

She watched the clock hands crawl around to ten-thirty. Everyone stopped work then, and got up and followed Mr Tyrell out into the hall. He opened a cupboard and took out a large torch.

'Is Frances coming with us?' Helen asked. 'She looks so tired.'

'She probably won't be able to keep up,' Claire said. 'And she'd make a noise and want to stop to look at things. I don't think she should come until she's more responsible.'

'Maybe she shouldn't go at all,' Aunt Loris said anxiously. 'She's had to adjust to a lot of new things today.'

'She needs the exercise,' said Mr Tyrell. 'And it's best that she learns to follow the same schedule as everyone else from the first.'

Frances, for all her tiredness, resented the way they talked, as though she were absent, or a person who spoke a different language.

'Go where?' she demanded. 'Why are you all putting on coats?' It's too late to go anywhere except bed.'

'What if she runs on ahead, or lags behind?' Claire said. 'I don't have to be in charge of her, do I?'

'Helen will take her,' Mr Tyrell said. 'But you can't all go together now that there are four of you. From now on you will have to be in pairs.'

Silently Helen handed her a short vinyl jacket from the hall cupboard, and all the girls put on woollen caps and gloves. Frances looked at their faces uneasily, sensing tension that bordered almost on fear. Mr Tyrell slid the bolts back on the front door and put the key in the lock.

'I never knew doors had to be unlocked from the inside,' Frances thought curiously.

There was a heavy screen door that also had to be unlocked from the inside, and then cold, dark air slashed in at them, causing Frances to plunge her hands deep into the coat pockets. There was a porch; a small yard rippling with wind-tossed, spiky bushes; a path glossy as fur with rain under light cast by a street lamp outside the front gate. It looked an ordinary suburban front garden. Mr Tyrell opened the gate a little, looked up and down the street, and then turned and beckoned. Frances stepped off the porch and was pulled back by Helen, but Rosgrana and Claire went out through the gate. Mr Tyrell didn't accompany them. He stood outside on the pavement and held something in the palm of his hand, studying it closely under the street lamp.

'What's he doing? Where did the girls go?' Frances whispered.

'We run every night for exercise. Father has a stopwatch. That's how he could tell if anything went wrong, anything unexpected, and he'd come and look for us. He knows how long it takes us to run the course he chose. When it's our turn, you must stay with me, and it's best to keep to the grass strips by the road. It's quieter.'

'Do we have to go?' Frances asked. 'I never go running. It seems mad, anyhow, in the dark like this.'

'It's important to keep healthy. And out there, slow down and walk normally, if we meet other people. If they ask us anything, I shall be the one to answer. Father decided what we should say if we're ever stopped. I'm to tell them we're out looking for a puppy who wandered off. And if they offer to help, and ask where they should return the pup if they find it, you mustn't point out this house. But we never do see anyone. Father chose this time because it isn't likely that there would be people about. And it's not so late that the sound of footsteps running by would be alarming.'

Frances, bewildered by the long day, waited with wire-taut nerves. Framed by the half-open gate, the dark street seemed almost sinister, filled with menacing, unseen things. She wanted to go back inside the house. When she felt that she couldn't stand one second more of the uneasy waiting, Rosgrana and Claire came back. 'Come on, it's our turn,' Helen whispered and took her hand and drew her out into the darkness on the other side of the gate.

It wasn't like running for exercise at all. It wasn't a game. Helen didn't speak, and clutched Frances's hand tightly as they ran along the deserted street. Frances was aware of unlit houses and buildings crouched like sleeping animals. Somewhere a dog barked at their passing, even though their feet made scarcely a sound on the grass nature-strip. Raindrops scattered from tired winter trees; the street was long and hushed and empty except for themselves, running.

They turned a corner, passed a park, a wild place of restless trees and rain. It stretched for the entire side of a block and around the corner into the next street. Sleeping houses blurred like smoke past her eyes. 'Don't stop,' Helen said breathlessly. 'We have to get back in time, or he'll come looking for us.'

There was a petrol station and a large building like a ship stranded in a black sea; a stretch of home units; another corner and rain, driven by a cold, keen wind, stinging at their faces. 'I can't run one more step,' Frances panted, fighting the agony of a stitch in her side. She hallucinated shadows into ogres, fancied that she could hear pounding footsteps behind them in the night. She clung to Helen's hand as though it were a lifeline.

'You can't stop. We're almost home,' Helen said.

A corner; a paling fence like a mouth of broken teeth; houses; a vacant block; a laneway flagged with bluestone blocks. And ahead, under the street lamp, she could see at last their front fence with the gate open, waiting for her like a haven. Home.

She reached it, stumbled through and fell to her knees, whimpering with pain and fear.

'It's all right, Frances,' Mr Tyrell said softly, reaching down and helping her to her feet. 'You're safe, my dear. Quite safe.'

Seven

On Sunday Mr Tyrell and Aunt Loris went to a temple meeting for adult members, and Rosgrana was left in charge of the house. She told Frances that no work was to be done unless it were strictly necessary, and she herself put aside her sewing and read in the sitting room. 'What will I do?' asked Frances. 'Can't you fix the television so we can watch it? Video, if you can't make the proper set work.' Even the video tapes, dull as they sounded from Claire's description, would be preferable to inactivity.

'You don't know anything. Sunday is for a day of rest. And Father wouldn't want you to see the video tapes yet. You wouldn't understand them. You'll have to study quietly on your own today. That's what we always do when Father's at the meeting.'

'Studying's not rest,' Frances said disagreeably.

'Only for people who find it difficult,' Clare said. 'After the war, when we start a new civilization, everyone should already know as much as they possibly can. You certainly won't be able to sit down and learn things then. There won't be any time.'

'There's a lot she doesn't know or understand,' Helen said, but didn't sound unkind like Claire. Rosgrana gave Frances some of the temple's religious instruction sheets, and Frances took them upstairs and made herself as comfortable as she could in the cold attic. She slipped under the blankets and wedged the two pillows as a back rest. Then she started to read, concentrating hard to find out just what it was that brought that engrossed look to Aunt Loris's face. She carefully read one page and thought that it sounded as hectoring as Mr Tyrell's prayer before meals, studded with grand-sounding words and admonitions to avoid evil. She persevered for several pages, sighed, and went back to the beginning. Soon she put the sheets of paper aside. There was something disturbing about their message, almost frightening.

She looked around the plain little room and wondered how Claire could bear it. It would be fun, she thought, if Claire were a different sort of girl, and they could make wonderful, crazy plans to redecorate it together. 'A mural,' she thought. 'We could paint a jungle mural all around the walls and over the ceiling. And we could get rid of that creepy-looking old wardrobe or paint it bright green. Something mad like that.'

There was scarcely any indication that Claire

even used the room. Her side of the chest of drawers was bare save for some pencils in a glass, and a writing pad. 'Studies even in her sleep,' Frances thought resentfully, aching suddenly for Kerry and her breezy, uncomplicated company. It was terrible that Kerry was so far away, across all those unfamiliar suburbs, and she hadn't been able to contact her yet to explain her sudden departure from school.

The telephone in that house was probably in the front room which Mr Tyrell used as his office, but perhaps there might be an extension upstairs. She didn't want to ask Rosgrana if she could use the phone, in case she said they weren't allowed to ring people on Sundays. She got out of bed and listened at the head of the stairs, but the girls were still in the living-room and the door was closed. Frances opened the door of Rosgrana's room.

It looked more like a workroom than a girl's bedroom. The overflow from the sewing table on the landing had found a place on the dressing table here. A cardboard dressmaker's model stood spookily in one corner, and although everything was arranged tidily, the room was just as depressing as the attic above. The window sill bore a row of carefully aligned reels of cotton. It was as though Rosgrana held no other interests except as seamstress for her family. There was certainly no telephone extension in this bleak room.

Frances went into Helen's room next door. The

lower window panes there' weren't made from frosted glass, but had been painted over with white matt paint. She was surprised and oddly disappointed to find that Helen kept her room even more fussily neat than Claire. The curtains, parted slightly to allow the entry of light through the clear panes below the ceiling, had been fastened to the window sill with several drawing pins. It was obvious that Helen didn't ever have the inclination to knot them impatiently as far out of the way as possible. There was nothing on her bedside table except a garden manual, a nail-file, comb and tiny mirror. The whole room was as impersonal and clean as a hospital foyer. It was just too immaculate.

Frances approached the window and tried to open it, but like the windows in the attic, this one couldn't be raised, either. A sudden, unexpected flash of colour caught her eye. Tucked away behind the left-hand curtain, as though Helen didn't want anyone to know that she owned anything so frivolous, there was a bright paper bird suspended on a thread. And someone had been scratching with a pin on the window ledge, and had tried, unsuccessfully, to erase the marks. Frances read the clumsy string of repeated letters. P.D. Paul. P. Drayton. Paul Drayton.

She heard the sound of the living-room door opening, and darted out to the landing. She sauntered innocently downstairs, and Helen gave her a quick, suspicious look as they passed each other. 'I got fed up with reading,' Frances said airily. 'I think I'll go outside for a bit.'

'Rosgrana has the keys. The doors have special locks that can't be opened from inside without a key. She won't be very pleased with you, wanting to go outside.'

'I don't see that it's such a big inconvenience, unlocking a door,' Frances said. 'It would only take her a couple of seconds.'

'She'll have to go out with you.'

'I never said I wanted her to.'

'You certainly won't be allowed out there without Rosgrana. There are special rules when Father isn't at home.'

Frances opened her mouth to say something derogatory about the house and its rules and everyone in it, and thought better of it. She looked at Helen, noticing her nails properly for the first time. They were raggedly bitten and ugly, and under her scrutiny, Helen blushed and put her hands behind her back. Frances, moved to pity by the fingernail biting, saw something in her eyes that she hadn't noticed before. Sadness? Loneliness?

'Stop staring at me like that,' Helen said sharply. 'It's rude to stare at people.'

'Listen, why don't you come outside with me? We could play something. Don't you get sick of hanging around inside? If you've got a ball, we could rig up a goal and play netball.'

'I don't know how to play that. I'm too old to play silly games, anyhow. I've never played such games.'

'Well, come outside anyway. Just for company.'

'I like my own company.'

Helen went into her bedroom and shut the door behind her. Frances looked at the closed door. She was certain that Helen had hesitated, just for a second or two, before shutting the door between them. Frances sighed, and went downstairs and asked Rosgrana if she could go outside.

'Not on your own,' said Rosgrana. 'I'd have to be with you. Why do you want to go out there? Why don't you sit down here with us and read? You can't have finished those papers I gave you, and it's important that you get through as much basic instruction as quickly as possible. And it's much too cold outside, anyhow.'

'I've got a terrible headache,' Frances lied glibly. 'My eyes hurt if I read too long.'

'Your aunt didn't tell us that.' Rosgrana sounded annoyed and even worried. 'You should have had your eyes attended to and glasses prescribed before you moved in here. It's not always possible . . . it's going to be inconvenient if you need glasses.'

'It's not that sort of eye-strain. We had our eyes checked at school last year. It's just a headache I get sometimes from reading. It'll clear away if I go outside in the fresh air. It always does.'

'I'll take you outside for five minutes and not any longer. Father doesn't like us to be outside when he's away at the temple.'

Rosgrana grudgingly unlocked the kitchen door and its screen. The day was not inviting. Great brooding clouds inched, slug like, across the flax-coloured sky, and the yard was wet with the night's rain. Frances hugged her arms across her chest for warmth and walked briskly down the length of the yard. She touched the padlock on the back gate.

'It's locked, of course,' Rosgrana said irritably. 'I locked it after Father took the van through. You certainly couldn't go for a walk out there, any-how.'

'You mean you don't even go for walks?'

'It's not possible. We don't need to, either. Father attends to everything necessary out there.'

Frances tilted her head back but still wasn't able to see over the strands of barbed wire slicing the melancholy sky. 'Who lives next door?' she asked.

'I don't know. We don't have anything to do with the people around here. And stop pushing against the fence like that. You'll make a noise, and somebody might hear you. Come back inside; it's far too cold and miserable out here.'

'My headache hasn't gone yet,' Frances said stubbornly. 'Can't you unlock the side gate to the front garden?'

'We aren't allowed out there under any circumstances, even when Father is home. It's too risky.

People would see us. It wasn't possible to seal the front garden from the street. It has to look like all the others.' Rosgrana's face was sharp and bad tempered with the cold. 'It's already been explained to you,' she said crossly. 'We don't want anyone at all knowing about us. People are terrible out there. Your aunt was different, because Father could tell at once that she was suitable. He was given permission by the council to contact her again after their first meeting and form a relationship. But we don't want anyone else in here with their evil ways. You're lucky Father let you come here to live, and you must do as you're told. And I'm telling you to come back inside at once. There's no reason to be out here, anyway. I hate it out here. It's not safe, like the house.'

She hustled Frances inside and locked the door and returned to the living-room. Frances stayed in the kitchen, mourning for Kerry's kindly house, where the doors, like arms, seemed always open to welcome people. 'I've got to talk to Kerry,' she thought longingly. 'There has to be a phone down here somewhere.'

She crept along the hall past the living-room and opened the door of Mr Tyrell's office. It was furnished with a large desk and typewriter, a duplicating machine and some metal filing cabinets. A telephone stood on the desk, but nowhere in that tidy office could she find a telephone directory. And she didn't know Kerry's number, because she'd never rung her before. She hunted all over the office for the directory. The desk drawers were locked and so was the filing cabinet, but surely Mr Tyrell wouldn't lock away such an ordinary thing as a telephone book? Frances gave up the search. She wandered back into the hall and stood there, feeling lost and miserable.

Suddenly, the front doorbell rang. The noise was so unexpected that she jumped, so used had she become to the habitual silence of the house. She went into the living room to get the key from Rosgrana to open the door to the visitor.

Rosgrana, Helen and Claire had put down their books and were sitting motionless. 'There's someone at the door,' Frances said, and was halted by the fierce look Rosgrana flung at her. The doorbell sounded again, more impatiently. Frances stared at the three girls, bewildered by their hesitation. They drew very close to Rosgrana, the custodian of the keys. They listened, their faces quite still, not turning to the direction of the sound, as though by such rejection they could hasten its departure. Helen gripped her book tightly; Claire put her hand into Rosgrana's. The person at the door rang twice more and footsteps paced across the porch and there was the distant sound of the front gate being slammed shut. Then silence.

After a few seconds the girls drew apart and picked up their books as though nothing had happened, but they seemed to Frances like birds, still ruffled and afraid even after the cat had left the garden. 'Why on earth didn't you answer the door?' she demanded.

'We never answer the door,' Rosgrana said. 'You mustn't ever make one sound if anyone comes to that door. They have to believe that nobody's home. If it's important, like the electricity being turned off for repairs, or something like that, they will leave a message of some kind in the letterbox, and Father will deal with it later.'

'They might have left one now. I'll run out and have a look,' Frances offered.

'No one's allowed out into the front garden. I already told you that. Father checks the letterbox each day.'

'We should have answered that door,' Frances persisted. 'Once when Aunt Loris and I were living in the flat, someone came around giving out free make-up samples. You didn't have to sign up to buy any, either. It was a sales promotion for a new brand. And it could have been someone like that just now at this front door. We don't know what we missed out on. You should have let me answer it, Rosgrana.'

'And you should know by now why we don't.' Rosgrana said curtly. 'We would never accept goods we hadn't paid for, either, especially not cosmetics. Father let us watch some advertisements on television once, to see how degrading it is. We don't use cosmetics. It would be very wrong.'

'I don't see anything bad about eye shadow and stuff like that.'

'Your mind is still cluttered with stupid ideas from out there,' Claire said.

'What's so stupid about wanting to look nice?' Frances demanded, annoyed. 'Helen would look terrific with eye shadow and her hair done differently. It looks so old fashioned yanked back like that.' She put out a hand and touched Helen's hair, and it felt as soft and silky as water. 'She should go and have it styled properly at a hairdresser's.'

'We don't go to places like that,' Helen said. She put Frances's hand away from her hair, but gently, not shrugging her off, as though to apologize for the shut door. 'The only times we ever go outside this house is for exercise at night and for the young people's meetings at the temple.'

'You must go out. The beach, skating . . . everyone does.'

'We don't,' Rosgrana said. 'We have a special job to do, and that's to prepare ourselves for the new world. You should forget all those useless things out there, Frances. All those other people and what they do don't really matter. They won't even be part of the new world, after this one is destroyed.'

Frances felt her mind bolt away, as it did every time any one of them mentioned that terrible war. But they were all so certain. So convinced. There was even pity in their eyes when they looked at her, as though she had been rescued from a wild and perilous sea. She'd been saved only by their stretching out a hand to her. And those hundreds of books in the study; people who had read so many books would be wise enough to distinguish truth from deception.

Frances made her mind stand at attention and examine the possibility of war, and whether the temple people knew how to survive it. And if it were true, her only hope, apparently, lay in trying to adapt to their strange way of doing things. Even to spending a school-holiday Sunday afternoon sitting in a room with people who didn't seem inclined to talk.

The afternoon seemed endless. Helen rested her head on her folded arms and fell asleep at the table. Claire and Rosgrana read. Frances sat in front of the heater and tried to do the same, but couldn't concentrate. She found, instead, that she was listening.

To sounds outside the house.

Listening very carefully, she could hear people walking along the footpath. Occasionally a car passed; a dog was barking in a nearby yard; far off, somebody was using an electric motor of some kind; branches stirred and shed waterdrops outside the shuttered windows.

Every sound seemed, in some mysterious way, important and meriting close attention.

Each sound seemed threatening.

She could sense that the girls, too, were listening and taking heed of the terrible, frightening sounds. Rosgrana would stop reading and listen to the footsteps passing the house, the dog barking. Helen, even though she appeared asleep, stirred restlessly every time a car passed. Claire remarked once that she wished she had her cardigan, that she wanted a drink of water, but she didn't leave the room to fetch either.

'They're frightened,' Frances thought. 'They're really scared, being in this house alone.' She watched them secretly over the top of her unread book. Their faces, as they listened, were impassive, but she knew that they were very frightened. They seemed to draw closer to one another at the table as the afternoon crawled on, and closer still, each time footsteps echoed along the pavement on the other side of the fence. And when early evening darkened the room, none of them moved to draw the curtains or switch on the light.

Frances gave up the pretence of reading. She thought of the long, high-ceilinged hallway, and the narrow staircase, and the shadows clustering all over the house. And outside, she thought nervously, all those strangers passing, and Aunt Loris not here, and Mr Tyrell not here.

She jumped up and went to sit with the others at the table, close to Rosgrana, the custodian of the keys. Fear lapped at her gently, like a tide nudging at a twig. She felt herself drawn into that tide, under it, engulfed. 'The war,' she thought frantically. 'It's not just an idea at all. It's going to happen really, and everyone outside is evil, everything is evil, and the only safe place is inside this house!'

When it was completely dark, they heard the sound of the van being driven down the laneway at the side of the house. 'Father's home,' Rosgrana said, in a voice almost strident with relief. 'I'll go and unlock the back gate.'

'He's late,' said Helen. 'It's always terrible when he's late. Sometimes the traffic is thick on Sundays, on that side of the city.'

'It probably wasn't the traffic at all,' Claire said spitefully. 'I expect that they were delayed at the temple because of Frances's aunt. It's always awkward when a stranger comes to join the temple. They'd have to keep stopping today, to explain things to her.'

But Frances didn't pay any attention to her malice. She was listening intently to the back door being opened, and Aunt Loris coming in, and last of all, locking the door behind him, locking out the shadows and the threats, Mr Tyrell. She ran across the room and caught hold of Mr Tyrell, as though she were drowning in that room swimming with green light.

'Someone came to the door!' she whispered. 'We were so scared! Oh, I'm so glad you're back. There were all these noises out there . . . I was so scared!'

She clung to his arm, and he seemed to her like a great, strong tree.

Eight

That night she woke up, fleeing terrified from a nightmare of people lying dead in the streets. All the buildings where her name had been scrawled in hidden places were shattered ruins, as though she had never lived anywhere. She sat up in bed and fought away the clutching tendrils of the dream. Moonlight, like melting ice, spilled in through the two clear panes at the top of the window. The floorboards looked as silvery cold as a rink. Claire, in the other bed, slept deeply, her face stern and remote, like a carved stone angel. Frances was afraid to go back to sleep because of the dream.

She'd dreamed that Kerry was buried beneath a great mound of broken bricks and plaster, and she had been trying to save Kerry, to dig her free from the debris. And Mr Tyrell had stood there watching, but he wouldn't help. 'That girl can't be saved,' he kept insisting. 'She doesn't belong to us. She wasn't chosen to be saved. There's no possible way you can help her, Frances.'

There had to be a way. What she must do, Frances thought, was to strive with all her power to learn as much about the temple as though she'd been a member since her birth. She would master every task they set her in the shortest possible time. And when she'd learned all she could, she would leave the house and go and persuade Kerry, and Kerry's family, to belong to the temple, too. And then Kerry would be safe.

Claire turned over neatly, scarcely disturbing the bedclothes. She breathed deeply in her safe, assured sleep, and Frances, lying awake till morning, envied her.

In the days following, she made an immense effort. She didn't say one word at mealtimes, and hung up her clothes neatly every time she changed. She accepted Rosgrana's orders without answering back or sulking, and stopped complaining about not being allowed in the back yard by herself. Aunt Loris looked at her approvingly at the end of each day, and Mr Tyrell told her that she had earned the right to learn a practical skill that would be of use to the temple council.

'Rosgrana can instruct you in basic typing,' he said. 'We still have the manual she used. You may use the study period each evening, and work at the typewriter in my office. I'm very pleased, Frances, that you seem to be making an effort to put your old life behind you and fit in with our ways.'

On the first night, Rosgrana showed her how

to place her fingers on the keyboard and which ones to use for the various letters. 'You must get each exercise perfect before you attempt the next one,' she said. 'Follow the exercises and don't waste paper. Use both sides.'

Frances discovered that she had a natural ability for typing. She sailed through the first three exercises and produced a twenty-line block with scarcely any errors. She began to play around with the keys, making up her own word combinations. 'This is great fun,' she said enthusiastically.

'It's not meant to be a game,' Rosgrana said, frowning. 'You are not to play the fool. There's always a lot of typing to be done for the temple council, and I can't do as much as I used to since I've taken over the sewing for this house. But you're not too young to learn. You must be sensible about it, right from the start, or I'll tell Father.'

Frances, subdued, paid attention to the set exercises in the manual. Rosgrana watched her critically for a while, and then left her to practise on her own. It was cold in the office, but Frances preferred it to being in the big room with all of them studying so ponderously. She knew that she had no chance whatever of surpassing Claire in any form of academic study. It was pleasant to find that at least she had the ability to touch type, and the delight she felt when she looked at each finished, perfect exercise soon turned into pride. She glanced through the manual at the timings Rosgrana had pencilled in when she'd been learning to type. Frances saw that Rosgrana's progress had been laborious and slow. She could do any of those exercises in a quarter of the time that Rosgrana had needed. It was marvellous to be smarter than one of the Tyrell girls, after having been made to feel so inferior. She looked at her pages with their neat thickets of correct words. 'I bet no other kid my age ever managed to learn typing so fast,' she thought triumphantly. 'I bet Claire couldn't.'

She was so smitten with success that she jumped up and took the completed work into the big room and showed it proudly to Mr Tyrell. 'I've finished right up to lesson seven already,' she boasted. 'Not one mistake. And Rosgrana didn't even have to show me anything after that half hour. I worked it out all by myself.'

Mr Tyrell didn't even glance at her work, and his face was suddenly cold and terrible. The girls looked up from their books and stared. 'I finished . . .' Frances said lamely, conscious that she was not, after all, in favour, and that she had somehow made a blunder. 'I just wanted to show . . '

'Father,' Helen said diffidently, 'Frances hasn't been here long enough to know that . . .'

Claire gave them both an incredulous, pitying look and went on with her studying, as one would ignore a prattling, attention-seeking child. Frances felt her cheeks redden with hot embarrass ment. Mr Tyrell's voice was no longer soft; it was iron hard with anger, and the anger was directed at her. Helen he ignored. 'You are never to intrude like that when we are working!' he said furiously. 'You know the rule about silence in the study time. You have most certainly been here long enough to know that. Bursting in here for praise, filled with vanity ... Naturally I expect you to work perfectly without supervision. It's the rule here for everyone.'

Frances looked to Aunt Loris for help, but her aunt regarded her soberly, as though she were ashamed of owning her. 'I'm sorry,' Frances said. 'I won't do it again.'

'You shouldn't have done it in the first place,' Mr Tyrell said coldly. 'You should have known.'

It seemed to her that every person in the house had flung that phrase at her since she had come there to live. Even her aunt. She felt again the appalling sensation that her aunt stood with the Tyrells on some far shore, and she'd never be able to reach them.

'The reading you have done should have taught you,' Mr Tyrell said. 'The instructions from the temple, it was all set down there, the things you aren't permitted to do. I thought you'd studied those leaflets properly. I'm not going to have you bring unacceptable behaviour into this house when my girls have been so carefully brought up!'

Frances kept her eyes down so she wouldn't have to look at the girls sitting there witnessing that savage telling off. Listening to her humiliation. Although, from under her eyelashes, she saw that Helen at least, had been charitable enough to leave the table and go to a bookcase at the far end of the room. Mr Tyrell's lecture went on and on. It was as though she had committed some dreadful crime, instead of just thoughtlessly rushing into the room to show off her work. No one had ever been so angry with her. She couldn't remember even one teacher speaking to her in such a way, glaring at her with such hostility.

'I'm sorry,' she mumbled when he finally stopped.

'Very well,' he said, his rage subsiding quite abruptly. 'You may go back to your work now.' He spoke in his normal voice, as though nothing had happened. It was odd, as though he were not really in charge of his own moods, and Frances crept away to the office, shaken by that inordinate public scolding. She even cried a little, because it seemed so impossible that she could ever measure up to the Tyrells' standards and learn to act correctly.

'Trying my best . . .' she muttered into the darkness of her folded arms. 'He's awful. I hate him . . . hate being here . . . it's too hard . . .' But even while saying that, she realized that she had no choice. She had to live as the temple decreed, or be killed in the war because she was not one of the chosen. It was futile to cry.

All the next week she strove to please. She

inspected the work roster each morning and hurried off to begin her part of the housework without having to be told. She studied the reading material from the temple and learned whole passages by heart. She paid respectful attention when Mr Tyrell said grace, and tried not to mind that Claire so obviously disliked having to share a room with her, and that the days were long and difficult and lonely. 'All that matters is being saved when the war comes,' she kept reminding herself. 'And getting Kerry to join the temple so she'll be safe, too. After the war, we can go away and live somewhere different from the Tyrells.'

Mr Tyrell allowed her to watch some of the video tapes, which turned out to be nothing more than televised lectures of what she had read already in the instruction sheets. And the people delivering the filmed lectures were just as authoritative and forbidding as Mr Tyrell. Accompanying the tapes were question sheets which had to be filled in afterwards. Frances secretly dreaded the video sessions, in case she missed a point that would be included in one of the questionnaires. Mr Tyrell obviously regarded the taped lectures and the testing as being of enormous importance.

But Frances did her best and Aunt Loris noticed that she was trying hard. 'I daresay you'll be allowed to come to a temple meeting soon, Frances,' she said. 'The council have been asking about you, and how your progress is coming along. Finley told them it was very encouraging.'

'Has he forgotten about the typing, then?' Frances asked.

'I don't suppose he's forgotten about it. But you haven't done anything like that again, and he realizes you've learned from your mistake. He doesn't hold grudges, if that's what you mean, but he'd never pardon the same mistake again. You want to be careful that you never barge in there again during study time to show him work you've done. You just wait till he asks to see it. He's in charge here.'

Frances remembered that chilling, savage voice telling her off.

'But you've been working hard lately and he's pleased with you,' Aunt Loris said. 'You can have a bit of time off now, if you like. You can go outside, seeing Helen's out there. Put these vegetable peelings on the compost heap while you're about it.'

Frances collected the basin of peelings from the sink, studying her aunt, and struck by the manner she adopted in the kitchen. Aunt Loris, engaged in household tasks, looked somehow exactly right, dignified even, as though the setting had been designed specially for her. Frances remembered all the rented flats they had lived in, and saw the contentment on her aunt's face, now that she had her own house.

There was something childlike about the contentment, almost like a little girl playing cubby house, but Frances looked at her aunt with new understanding. 'I mustn't do anything that would spoil it for her,' she thought as she took the peelings down to the compost heap. 'I've just got to fit in.'

Helen was sitting by the garden plot with her bright hair draped over a towel. 'I never realized it was so long,' Frances said, awed. 'It's fantastic! It must have taken ages to grow as long as that.'

'It's a nuisance to get dry in the winter,' Helen said, shrugging away the admiration. 'I'd rather . . .'

'What?' asked Frances. She noticed that Helen kept a careful watch on the back door, and even lowered her voice markedly before she answered.

'I'd much rather have it short,' Helen said. 'But they made me grow it, ever since I was ten. It used to grow in curls all over my head, but they decided it looked wrong for our way of life.' Close to her head, her hair still rippled in elegant waves, before the weight of her hair tugged them into straightness.

'It seems a shame to have to tie it back,' Frances said.

'I can't have it hanging about my face all the time. I'd never get any work done. You'll probably have to grow yours long, too, and plait it. The council decides matters like that. When you start going to meetings, they're sure to make you get rid of those curls.'

'Some poky old council telling me how I have

to do my hair!' Frances thought indignantly. 'I'd just like to see them try!' And then she remembered abruptly that the council could look into the future and had seen the war coming, and knew what people must do to be saved. Perhaps when they saw her, they would take one look at her riotous red hair and decide that even growing it long and plaiting it neatly out of the way wouldn't save her. They would see with one glance that she didn't look anything like the Tyrell girls and never would. 'Do they ever send anyone away?' she asked Helen. 'Tell them that they can't go on living in a temple house any more because they're not suitable?'

'Everyone takes good care to be suitable. Who would want to die out there in the war?' Helen ran her hands through her hair and began to twist it back into a single plait.

'Let me do it,' Frances said. It was a waste, she thought, having wonderful hair the colour of new copper, and nobody ever saw it. Nobody except the Tyrell family and the people at the temple. Holding the comb, she realized that as far as she knew, Helen, Rosgrana and Claire had never met anyone else apart from the temple followers.

'Please be quick,' said Helen. 'I've been out here for too long. Father doesn't like it if we sit about during the day doing nothing. He's going to ask me have I done this and have I done that, and I want to be able to say yes, I've finished. Less trouble if you can say yes, you've finished. Do hurry, Frances. It doesn't matter how it looks, as long as it's neat.'

Frances twisted the rubber band on the end of the long plait. It looked tidy and modest, unlike her own hair. 'So you reckon that when the council gets around to seeing me, they'll be angry about my hair?' she asked.

'Not angry. Concerned. They'll say that you must grow it long and tie it back, to get rid of the curliness. You'll have to obey their decision.' Again there was the wary, darting glance at the back door. 'Just as I did, when they said I was too young to leave this house and work at the market garden,' Helen blurted. 'That's one of the properties the temple owns. It supplies all the fruit and vegetables for the staff at the temple. I would have loved it, working outside all the time. But they wouldn't let me go.'

Frances saw again the fleeting, buried sadness in her eyes. 'I think it's mad that they wouldn't let you,' she said. 'Specially as you're so good at gardening and like it so much. Why didn't you just make a big fuss till they let you?'

'That wouldn't have been any use. It would have only proved to them that I was too young, if I'd set about throwing a tantrum. And they're stricter now, about someone my age living away from their family. A friend, someone I knew from meetings, was allowed to work at the market garden, but it hasn't been successful. I think there's going to be serious trouble. Everything has gone wrong, and Paul . . .'

She stopped quickly and got up. 'You'll have to come inside now,' she said, nervously gathering up the towel and comb. 'You can't be out here on your own. I wasn't supposed to be, really. It was only that I'd washed my hair and needed to get it dry.'

But Frances, without even being aware of doing so, had started towards the house. 'I'm learning,' she thought, pleased. 'I really am learning. I remembered the rule without being told.'

Nine

Aunt Loris told her that she was to attend a temple meeting on the following Wednesday. 'I'm very pleased that Finley's allowing you to go, Frances,' she said. 'It means that he thinks you're fitting into this family at last. And if the council is pleased with you on Wednesday, you'll be able to attend the young people's meetings with Rosgrana and Claire and Helen from now on.'

Frances was anxious to make a good impression at the temple from the first. She didn't want the council to tell her that her hair was unsuitable, so she took a pair of scissors from Rosgrana's sewing table.

It wasn't easy to find the time to get rid of her curls. Rosgrana decided that the living room should be cleaned thoroughly, which meant that the hundreds of books had to be removed from the shelves and dusted. Frances was kept busy for a couple of days. The chairs were covered with sheets and the curtains taken down and laundered. At first the job seemed a welcome break in the usual boring cycle of housework. The books stood like a miniature city of skyscrapers all over the floor; it was almost fun, as though they were caught up in the excitement of moving house or redecorating. Frances found herself whistling as she dusted each book.

'Don't make that noise,' Rosgrana ordered sharply.

'Why not? I'm only whistling.'

'Sounds carry when there aren't curtains up on the windows. And I'd prefer that you gave all your attention to those books. If a job is worth doing, it's worth doing properly.'

Frances wished that she and Helen had been left alone to clean out the big room. Helen was always reserved when the rest of her family was about, but sometimes, when Rosgrana was being particularly bossy and overbearing, Helen would catch Frances's eye and half-smile, or gently raise an eyebrow.

The sorting of the books soon palled, with their disagreeable smell of old paper and binding. Frances looked hopefully at the titles, but there was nothing she would choose just for the sheer pleasure of reading. And Rosgrana's presence made the task just another formidable chore which must be done thoroughly and not skimped. At last she finished dusting and began to return the books to the newly polished shelves. She made a mess of it. 'They have labels on the spines,' Rosgrana scolded her irritably. 'You have to put them back according to the labels. Surely you can do such a simple task properly!'

Frances knew she should have realized that there would certainly be some sort of book-filing system in this meticulous household. She'd been replacing the books according to size, but had to take them all down and start again.

'You'd better go upstairs and wash before dinner,' Rosgrana said. 'You're covered in dust. You could have your bath now and wash your hair because of the meeting tomorrow. And please try to comb your hair so that it will dry flat and not look such a mess.'

While the bath water was running, Frances took the scissors out of her pocket and began to cut off all her curls, anxious to transform her hair into a neat bob that would show willingness to comply with the rules of the temple council. The curls fell into the basin like a shower of springy little question marks. It was more difficult than she'd imagined, to get both sides an even length. Her hair, after a lot of indiscriminate snipping, looked almost straight, but it certainly didn't sit in a neat cap like a professional cut. She inspected it doubtfully in the mirror, and then had a bath, and washed her hair. Afterwards she cleaned up the bathroom, wrapping the shorn hair in paper and putting it into the wastepaper basket. It was becoming a habit now, cleaning up after her as she went through the day, because it was much easier than being constantly reproved.

She dressed, and combed what was left of her hair. It was drastically shorter than she'd intended and stuck up in odd wisps, but there was no trace of a curl, and she felt pleased with the result. Tomorrow at the temple, the council would surely find no fault with her. It was the sort of haircut adopted by people who were training for squad swimming. It made her feel confident and slightly swaggering, as though she'd won a row of trophies. She went downstairs to help set the table for dinner.

The girls looked up and stared. 'I did it myself,' Frances said proudly. 'Quicker than growing it long and plaiting it. That would take years. It was easier just chopping off all those curls.'

'But we don't wear our hair cut short like boys!' Claire said. 'It's against the rules. You shouldn't have done it.'

Frances glanced at her quickly, to see if she were just being spiteful, but Claire looked genuinely concerned. 'You really shouldn't have cut it,' she said. 'You won't be able to go to any temple meetings until you've got it down to your shoulders again.'

'It looks absolutely terrible,' Rosgrana said coldly. 'Why didn't you ask someone about it first? You're too fond of taking things into your own hands. It's out of the question that you can go along to the meeting tomorrow looking like that.'

Frances felt almost sick with disappointment.

'But that's why I did it!' she wailed. 'I wasn't just fooling around. It was to get my hair looking right, for that meeting. Helen said she had to grow hers long to get rid of the curl, and this was just a sort of time-saving thing that I did. If I told the council why I did it, they'd understand, wouldn't they?'

'You wouldn't be allowed in the temple looking like that,' Claire said.

'I doubt if you'll even be allowed to come to the table for dinner,' Rosgrana said. 'You had better put on a cap or a scarf or something. I don't know what Father's going to say.'

Mr Tyrell was just an ordinary person, Frances tried to reassure herself, knowing that he wasn't anything of the sort. She remembered his alarming voice, telling her off about the typing. In this house he was an absolute power, as strong as any dictator.

'I don't know what we're going to do about you, Frances,' Aunt Loris said, and she looked almost as uneasy as Frances felt. Clearly there was no help to be had there. 'How could you do such a silly thing? I should have thought you'd know better than cut your hair. If the girls aren't allowed to wear jeans, and you knew that, then it follows they wouldn't be allowed to have their hair cut off short like a boy, either. It's a shame. I was looking forward to taking you to the temple tomorrow. It would have made it seem as though you're properly one of us.'

112

'I don't know why everyone is scolding Frances,' Helen said abruptly. 'It was really my fault, anyhow. It was something I said and she misunderstood. Frances, you go back upstairs and stay there until it's sorted out. I'll explain to Father. Go on, it will be all right.'

Frances hurried thankfully away from their shocked reaction.

She lay on her bed and thought of her old life, when she and Aunt Loris had lived in flats and nothing more complicated than being a bit late with the rent had ever arisen. Things had been difficult at times, but not nearly as tough as life here. For all Aunt Loris's delight in fussing around the rooms with such an air of ownership, it still wasn't her house and never would be. It belonged utterly to the Tyrells, as though their name was fired on every brick.

As far as she could see, there were three things that could happen. The first was that by some miracle all the temple teachings would be made clear to her and she would be able to accept them without any reservations. And then she would fit in easily with the Tyrells and she would be saved in that war.

The second was that she'd never fit in at all, and the Tyrells would be told by the council to send her back to the ordinary world to live. And she would die when the war came.

And the third was that the war would never

happen at all, and that the people who believed in it were mistaken, and wasting their lives. All for nothing.

At that she sat upright. 'Of course it's true, what they believe,' she thought, frightened. 'Aunt Loris wouldn't have come here to live if it wasn't. That council, she must have met them at the temple, and watched them seeing into the future, and she'd know if they were faking. And she stays here and puts up with all this because she knows it's got to be like it is. It must be true.'

From the kitchen she could hear the sound of plates as her aunt dished up the meal. 'All that food down there in the basement,' she thought. 'The trouble he's gone to. Mr Tyrell would know for sure if it was true about the war coming. No one could cheat Mr Tyrell. He'd know straight away. It's going to happen all right, and if I'm not careful, I'm going to be sent away outside.'

When she thought she couldn't bear it one minute longer, sitting by herself in the dark with her crazy spinning thoughts and hunger, Helen came upstairs bearing food. 'You'd better eat this in my room,' she said. 'Claire will tell if she comes upstairs for anything. I can't stay, no one knows I'm up here. But there's no need to look so frightened. He was angry, and he won't let you come down for dinner or be down there at all tonight, as a punishment. It's to teach you not to do things without asking first. He wouldn't listen when I told him it was my fault. But I managed to get some food for you, before your aunt served up. I hid it in the laundry, that's why it's so cold. Hide the plates under my bed when you finish. Claire is forever running to Father with tales.'

Frances was hungry enough not to mind that the food was cold. Helen had even managed to put aside some dessert for her. Frances finished the meat and vegetables and bit into the square of baked bread pudding, which had become crust hard from its time in the cold laundry.

She picked up the small mirror from Helen's bedside table and studied her reflection and thought miserably that her short hair didn't look rakish and sporty any more. It looked, she thought, like the cropped head of a prisoner. She tugged, without much hope, at the painted window, but like all the windows in the house, it was sealed shut, with nails driven at an angle into the frame. There was a thin wire running down the length of the frame, taped into place. The alarm system. Aunt Loris had shown her that downstairs. Even if you managed to prise the nails out, the alarm would ring as soon as you tried to raise the window. There was no way to open it for fresh air.

She bit into the last crust of bread. There was a small sharp crunching sound, and a dislodged filling split away from one of her back teeth. 'Dentist,' Frances thought angrily. 'On top of everything else, a trip to the dentist.'

It was impossible to leave the tooth alone,

knowing that a filling had come loose. She slid the empty plates under Helen's bed and inspected her tooth in the mirror. The cavity left by the filling looked enormous, and had a razor sharp edge which ran right down into the gumline. 'I should go and tell Aunt Loris,' she thought, but the idea of facing Mr Tyrell with her shorn hair kept her sitting right where she was. She would tell Aunt Loris in the morning.

Suddenly she felt more cheerful than she had since they'd moved there to live. Aunt Loris would let her go back to Dr Morris, who had been their dentist for three years, in spite of all their moving around. And his surgery was just around the corner from where Kerry lived. Tomorrow she would be able to see Kerry! She ran her hands through her short hair. It didn't really look like a prisoner's, she thought happily. It felt like a holiday haircut, like someone setting off for a long summer holiday.

Outside the window, something landed and wove back and forth along the ledge. Frances saw by the silhouette that it was a cat. It seemed to know perfectly well that someone was on her side of the panes, and tapped the glass imperiously, wanting to come in. It purred and called to her from the other side, and then leaped out of sight, but she could still hear its muffled cry. She went out on the landing and stood there, listening.

Rosgrana's sewing table, with its attached cabinet of drawers, took up one wall. She could hear, more distinctly and much closer, the cat mewing behind there. She tugged the cabinet part forward, and found behind it a tiny leadlight window, only as big as a shoebox, set into the wall. She pushed at the latch, not really expecting it to move. This window, like all the windows in the house, would surely be sealed tightly. But the little window, overlooked perhaps because of its minute size, or because of being tucked away behind Rosgrana's work cabinet, opened easily.

The cat, a self-confident tabby with jade, slanted eyes, peered in at her. It had somehow found the window in a dense curtain of ivy and clematis and other tangled creepers. Nobody passing in the street would guess there was a tiny window there.

Frances carried the cat into Helen's room where it sat on the bed and washed itself, wetting a paw to dab fastidiously behind its ear. Frances was charmed by it. It was well past the kitten stage, and disinterested in the bit of cotton she dangled in front of its nose. It just sat and gazed at her with calm, independent eyes. Its colouring was unusual for a tabby; the coat between the stripes was a delicate coffee cream, and each individual hair was tipped with bronze. Frances thought it was the most beautiful cat she had ever seen, and wondered if it were a stray, and if she'd be allowed to keep it. It certainly wasn't a good time to ask, when everyone was so angry at her.

She shut the door of Helen's room and tiptoed

downstairs to the kitchen while everyone was in the big room studying. She poured some milk into a cup. There was a bowl of raw minced beef in the fridge, and she scooped up a handful and crept back upstairs. The cat, smelling food, wove impatient arabesques around her ankles. Frances put the food into the plates she'd eaten from earlier. The cat ate with aristocratic manners, and then folded into a neat sphinx on the bed and went to sleep.

She was immensely comforted by its presence. Aunt Loris had never let her encourage stray cats because she disliked them as pets. Frances thought that Mr Tyrell was probably the same; he certainly didn't seem the type of person who would welcome animals about the house. It would be better to get one of his daughters to ask permission; Claire, who was so obviously his favourite.

Fussing over the cat had made her forget her uncomfortable tooth, which was starting to hurt where the jagged edge ran into the gumline. If she had to have that tooth out, it would be a good time then to ask if she could keep the cat; when she came back from Dr Morris with her mouth filled up with cotton-wool packing. Everyone always felt sorry for people who'd come from the dentist.

But the cat appeared to have a defined lifestyle already. The sound of Mr Tyrell opening the front door to let the girls out for their exercise run woke the cat up. It mewed softly and jumped off the bed, and went out onto the landing. Frances plunged after it to stop it running downstairs, but it went straight to the little leadlight window and whisked through.

Frances called after it, but it didn't come back. She left the small window open so it could get in again whenever it wished, and moved Rosgrana's sewing table forward a little. Nobody would notice the draught on the landing, because the whole house was so cold. Apparently they hadn't even noticed the window, either. Nobody in that house, as far as she could see, ever as much as glanced at a window, or even thought about opening one. Which showed, she thought drearily, how much further they were along the path to salvation than she was.

She wished that she could fling open every window in the house and take great breaths of fresh air. Even if it was polluted, as the instruction books said, with all the massed evil in the world.

Ten

Next morning Claire ostentatiously got ready for the temple. She plaited her long hair, fussing to get it perfect, as though to underline the reason why Frances, through her own silliness, had to stay home. And because Mr Tyrell wouldn't allow her to stay in the house alone, Aunt Loris had to miss the meeting, too, to stay home with her. Frances waited impatiently for Mr Tyrell to take the girls to the temple, so she could tell her aunt about the tooth. She could even bear the thought of the dentist, because she should be able to see Kerry. As soon as she heard the van leave, she ran downstairs lightly, in spite of the aching tooth.

'What on earth's the matter with your face, all swollen up like that?' said Aunt Loris. 'Come here and let me look.'

Frances was gratified to know that the amount of pain she was feeling bore tangible evidence. She opened her mouth to show the gum, swollen and fiery, around the base of the broken tooth.

'That's just one of your first teeth,' Aunt Loris

said. 'If it's loose, maybe you can work it out by itself.'

'I already tried, and it's not loose at all. And it's too sore to touch, now. It's hurting worse every minute.'

'I don't know what arrangements Finley's made about trips to the dentist.'

'You can take me to Dr Morris, can't you? Or I could go by myself, though I don't know how to get back to Scully Road. You'd have to write down which trains and trams to get.'

'That's out of the question. We have to wait till Finley gets back from the temple with the girls. I have to know what he thinks. Why didn't you show up for breakfast and say you had tooth-ache?'

'I was too scared of what he'd say about my hair,' Frances said. 'And I just took it for granted you and I could go back and see Dr Morris while they were all at the meeting.'

'There you go again,' Aunt Loris said crossly. 'Rushing in without thinking. People don't go in and out of this house casually, as though it's a boarding house. Finley decides if it's safe or not. He's got the keys, so we can't get the doors open from this side, anyhow.'

'What? You mean we're locked in here? That's just terrible . . . he always leaves the keys with Rosgrana when he goes out with you. If she's allowed to have the keys, then you should, too. You're his wife.' Frances was angry and indignant on her aunt's behalf, but Aunt Loris didn't seem to mind at all, or even consider it an insult.

'Goodness me, Frances, I'm glad not to have the responsibility of those keys. I could just as easy put them down some place and not remember where. Rosgrana's used to looking after important things like that.'

'I've got to sit round with an abscessed tooth, just because we can't get out!'

'Then you should have said something at breakfast. Anyhow, you can surely put up with a bit of toothache until they come back. You'll just have to take a couple of aspros. And a hot-water bottle might get the swelling down a bit.'

Aggrieved, Frances sat at the kitchen table with her throbbing cheek pressed against a hot-water bottle. Every time she glanced at the locked door her annoyance grew. Aunt Loris got down on her hands and knees and buffed each separate linoleum tile to a brilliant gloss.

'What if I got appendicitis while they're out and the door was locked?' Frances demanded. 'Would I just have to stay here, and die in agony maybe, before he got back?'

'Don't be so silly. As if anything like that would happen outside your imagination. Anyhow, the doors are locked up like that so no one can break in. That's the main thing, no one can get in here while Finley's away. This house is like a fortress. I think it's a good, safe feeling, knowing that.'

'I don't. If you ask me, it's exactly like being a prisoner.'

Aunt Loris's face collapsed with anger. 'Don't you ever say that again!' she cried furiously. 'Even for a joke, I won't have you speak that way! It's not like a prison at all, this house. It's a privilege to live here. You're a stupid girl. How dare you come out with an insulting remark like that? It's a slur on me, that's what it is, hinting that I'm not clever enough to know the difference between a prison and a refuge!'

Frances had never seen her aunt so upset, and it was terrible, knowing that she'd caused it. She stared at the two clear panes of glass set above the window, just below the ceiling. The sky was a pure, clear blue, and as she watched, a distant flock of birds sped from one side to the other. It was almost unbearable, watching that far away, unhampered flight, when she was locked up inside the house.

Driven by pain, she got up and went to the window and tried to see through the lower panes. They were made of opaque, textured glass, like her bedroom window. It was like looking into the centre of a cloud.

'I'm sorry, Aunt Loris,' she said miserably. 'I don't mean it to come out sounding like that. Of course I understand why the doors have to be locked, and I know we're lucky to be living here. Can I have some more aspirin for this awful pain?'

Aunt Loris relented a little and had another look at the tooth under the electric light. 'Aspirin's not really going to do much good,' she said. 'Not now. You'll just have to cope with it till Finley gets back. I'll make you a cup of tea.'

It was nearly impossible to drink the tea, because of the devastating pain, but it was comforting to just sit there and hold the cup, knowing that the tea had been made specially for her. Frances snatched forlornly at the small solicitude, and felt that perhaps Aunt Loris had momentarily returned from that far shore, and still cared about her.

'Maybe I won't have to have it out,' she said hopefully. 'Dr Morris might be able to fill it again.'

'If it's an abscess, the tooth will have to come out. And it won't be Dr Morris. We couldn't go all the way back there. We could meet someone we knew, and that wouldn't do at all. They'd be asking questions, where we live, things like that. Finley will drive you to someone else, soon as he gets back.'

Frances was filled with dread. She knew that she was stupid about going to the dentist, but Dr Morris was used to her fear and knew how to soothe it away. She didn't think she could bear having a stranger extracting one of her teeth, particularly if Mr Tyrell was going to be there in the waiting room, overhearing the sounds of her cowardice.

'It'll be over fast,' Aunt Loris said briskly. 'There's no need to look so stricken. You can treat it as a sort of test, see, to show your uncle that you can stand up to hardship, just as good as his girls. It'll make up for you being so daft about your hair. Anyhow, there's no choice. You've got to behave at the dentist so as not to draw attention to yourself.'

Which was exactly what Mr Tyrell said to her when he came back from the temple meeting. 'It's vital that you don't make a fuss there,' he said. 'I can't stress how important it is. We can't have anyone outside the house noticing us particularly and becoming curious.'

She could tell that he wasn't pleased about her tooth needing urgent treatment. He and Rosgrana held a whispered consultation, glancing at her, then he went into his office to use the phone.

'Aunty, can't you come with me?' Frances begged, while he was making the call.

'Father said it would be better if he took you by himself,' Rosgrana said quickly. 'More than one person there with you would only attract attention.'

'But . . .'

'It's high time you got over being so neurotic at the dentist,' Aunt Loris said. 'You do everything your Uncle Finley says to. You've got to act differently now. You're expected to.' Aunt Loris didn't meet her eyes, and busied herself putting away the polishing gear. Frances buttoned up her jacket with fingers that trembled.

'I found a dentist who can attend to her straight away,' Mr Tyrell said, shutting the door of his office.

'I could come with her,' Helen said from the stairs where she had been standing quietly and watching without comment. 'Father, wouldn't it be better, seeing she's so nervous?'

'Don't be foolish, Helen,' said Mr Tyrell. 'A tooth extraction is nothing to be nervous about. Frances is going to be well behaved and sensible.'

Frances followed him numbly outside and got into the van. Rosgrana went through the business of unlocking the gate to the back fence and relocking it once he'd driven the van through. Mr Tyrell drove carefully out of the alley into the street.

'There are some things I want you to memorize carefully,' he said. 'Your name for the next hour or so will be Margaret James. If they ask you which dentist you visited before, you're to pretend that we're from Sydney. It's extremely important. Understand?'

Groggy with pain, she nodded. The aching had travelled along her jawline to reach her ear. She laid one gloved hand over the pain and shut her eyes. 'Why do I have to tell them that?' she asked.

'We never let anyone outside know the people who live in our house. Dentists keep records, and it's vital that our names never appear on any records whatsoever. And that of course applies to you, now that you live in my house. It will be better if you don't speak at all when we reach the surgery. I'll tell them everything they need to know. Understand, Margaret?'

She felt so quenched by pain that she wanted to stay for ever in the darkness behind her closed eyes. 'All right,' she said dully.

Mr Tyrell drove at a slow, careful pace through a network of streets until they came to a shopping centre. He parked the van and led Frances across the parking lot to the dental surgery. The cold air clawed at her throbbing face and she gasped, burrowing deep down inside her jacket collar. Mr Tyrell steered her up a flight of steps and into a waiting room. Frances groped for a chair and huddled there, thankful that he was explaining to the nurse at the desk and that she didn't have to say anything. She thought she would cry if she had to speak to anyone through the grinding pain.

'There's a form to be filled out for new patients,' the nurse said. 'Dr Kennicott won't be long. You were lucky we happened to have a cancellation. Your little girl can go in as soon as we finish with the last patient.'

Mr Tyrell sat in the chair next to Frances and filled in the form. Frances watched him print, in neat capital letters, the information required — Margaret James, aged 12, Flat 6/321 Charlton Street, Wakefield. In the space for a telephone number, he made a dash. 'But we've got . . .'

Frances said stupidly and shut up, meeting the smile that didn't travel as far as his eyes.

He handed the form back to the nurse. 'I'd like to settle the payment on this visit,' he said. 'I explained that we're from interstate and may not be staying in this area for very long. Would you have the account ready, please, when the dentist has attended to my daughter?'

Frances was holding herself as carefully as though she were made of crystal. She listened to the sound of the drill on the other side of the door and tried desperately to think of other things; Kerry, and how they had both managed to get enough courage to jump off the high diving board at the council pool last summer. There was the same sickening feeling in the pit of her stomach now.

'I'll come into the surgery with her, if you don't mind,' Mr Tyrell said smoothly. 'She co-operates much better if I stay with her.'

'Dr Kennicott really prefers that parents ...' said the nurse, but when the last patient was dismissed, Mr Tyrell stepped past her, holding Frances by the hand. He helped her into the chair, as though she were a very small child, and stood back out of the way behind the dentist. Frances looked at him, and he wasn't smiling at her now. There was no need, because she was the only person who could see his face, and it was cold and fierce and compelling. She was too afraid of him to give way to her usual panic.

The dentist made a routine check and the nurse filled in the details on the clean new card with the name that wasn't hers on the top. He made professionally kind, soothing remarks, calling her Margaret, which made her feel eerie, as though another person altogether was submitting to all this. There was the sting of the injection, and she clamped her eyes shut until the dentist had removed her tooth. 'It wasn't as dramatic as it looked,' he was saying to Mr Tyrell. 'The nerve was exposed, but there's no infection. Good thing that it's out. It will give the second molar plenty of room to come through. I'll only have to see her again if there's still any discomfort after twenty-four hours. That's the girl, Margaret. It's all over now, and you can get down.'

'Thank you,' Frances mumbled through the cotton wool. Dr Morris would have been proud of her, she thought, sitting through all that without a murmur. Only it had been due to Mr Tyrell's foreboding presence, not to any bravery on her part.

Mr Tyrell paid the account at the desk. 'Feel okay, now?' the nurse said, smiling at Frances. 'There wasn't any need for your Dad to be in there with you, was there? You were as good as gold. And I've just realized, looking at the address on your card, you're a neighbour of mine. How about that?'

Mr Tyrell's grip on Frances's hand tightened slightly. Frances looked from him to the nurse in consternation, not knowing how to handle things. 'Flat 6, 321 Charlton Street,' said the nurse. 'I just moved into that end of Charlton Street myself. I'm in number 311, in the villa units with the green tile roofs. Fancy us being neighbours.'

'Quite a coincidence,' murmured Mr Tyrell. 'But ours is only a temporary stay. I hope to find a suitable house for sale this weekend, over the other side of town. Closer to my firm.'

'We're sorry to be losing such a star patient.'

'And I certainly hope we can find such obliging dental services in our new suburb,' said Mr Tyrell. He walked Frances out of the surgery and down the stairs, letting her go only when they reached the van. He drove back by a different route and stopped the van in Charlton Street to check the numbers on the gate posts. 319 was a large block of flats, and 321 a smaller block.

'Just as well. She would have thought it a bit funny if 321 had been a shop or wasn't there at all,' Frances said indistinctly around the cotton-wool plug in her mouth and the numbness left by the injection.

'I should have checked beforehand, of course,' Mr Tyrell said. 'I chose this street from memory because I knew it contained a lot of flats. This will show you how careful we have to be at all times, Frances. One little error could cause people to be very inquisitive. Not that it would have mattered a great deal in this case, because we won't see that dentist again. There's no way he could possibly trace us.'

He made a U-turn in the street, and said, quite kindly, 'You'll be glad to get back to the house after this unpleasant little excursion.'

Frances was looking at the houses in the streets as they passed. A boy and a girl were walking hand in hand along a pavement. The girl was wearing a red wool cap with pom poms and red mittens. Someone was raking leaves into a pile in a front garden and whistling. Red and gold leaves spiralled away like a host of bright butterflies as a dog charged through the pile. Two girls, about the age of herself and Claire, called cheerfully from an upstairs window to someone below. A woman was tending a cluster of pot plants by her front gate. A very old man walked along the foot-path and raised his hat to her in a beautiful old-fashioned gesture.

Frances looked at patient cats on front-door steps waiting for homecoming owners; a front door painted endearingly and crazily with huge yellow daisies; windchimes swaying in an open window; open gates; curtains billowing softly at open windows; lawns coming right to the footpath with no fences at all; front doors wide, wide open.

'It will be good to get home,' said Mr Tyrell, but Frances didn't answer.

Eleven

When she finished being sick, she rinsed out her mouth and put in a fresh plug of cotton wool. She was always sick after a visit to the dentist. She knew that she would be perfectly all right now. It was unpleasant having cotton wool in her mouth as a reminder, but she dared not remove it altogether. It had been horrible enough taking out the old dressing and glimpsing the site of the extraction.

'Are you all right?' Helen asked at the bathroom door, but her voice sounded curt and unfriendly, as though she didn't care that Frances had been through an ordeal. Frances saw in the mirror that Helen's eyes were filled with some personal distress. She had been crying to such an extent that she looked almost ugly as she splashed cold water on her face.

'What's the matter?' Frances demanded.

'It was something they announced at the temple this morning, but I don't want to talk about it. But something I do want to talk about is that window on the landing. It must have been you who found it and left it open. And those bowls under my bed, with milk in one of them. You've been feeding that cat, haven't you?'

'How did you know about the cat?'

'I've heard it mewing outside, on my window ledge. Father will be angry if he finds out you gave good food to a cat. It's fortunate that I found those bowls, and not Claire. She would have told.'

'I was going to ask your Dad if we could keep it,' Frances said.

Helen looked at her scornfully. 'We're not allowed to have pets. It's against the temple rules, and you'd better not mention that you brought that cat inside. Rosgrana would be up here scrubbing down all the floors with disinfectant. She believes cats and dogs and animals like that can sap your energy. It's written somewhere in the instruction sheets from the temple. I tried to read that section once, but I couldn't understand it. I'm not as clever as Rosgrana.'

'Clever, nothing. It sounds like a lot of rubbish. That cat was gorgeous. I bet if Rosgrana saw it she'd want it just as much as I do.'

'Frances, you must understand that you'll never be allowed to have it as a pet. The best thing to do is to forget about it and never open that little window again in case it comes back inside.'

'But it's worth a try, asking,' Frances protested. 'All he can do is say no.'

'Is it? Once I found a canary in the yard, and

I caught it with my apron and brought it inside,' Helen said. 'It was really tame. It sat on my finger and ate breadcrumbs out of my hand. I would have loved to keep that little bird. I could have made a cage somehow, there's plenty of metal and wire down in the basement. But he wouldn't let me.'

'You should have just stood up to him and made him let you keep it.'

'No one makes him do things. He owns this house and everything in it.'

'He doesn't own me,' Frances said sharply.

'You'll only make things hard for yourself if you believe that. The temple says that every house must have a strong leader with all the power.' Helen dried her face and turned away to go downstairs. 'There's no reason why you can't come down, now,' she said. 'Father says you aren't to have special privileges just because you've been used to them in your other life. You aren't allowed to give into a little amount of discomfort. That tooth must be perfectly all right by now. Only, downstairs, don't tell anyone that I was in my room crying. Please, Frances.'

'I wouldn't. And what happened about the little bird? If he didn't let you keep it here, who did you give it to? The temple?'

'There aren't any birds at the temple. He killed it,' Helen said without any emotion. 'He just crushed it in his hand and killed it.'

Frances sat at the dinner table, making a pretence of eating the food put in front of her. She thought of the pleasant houses they had passed on the way home from the dentist. The girl walking hand in hand with the boy had looked a little like Helen. Her long hair had swung like a bright banner from under that cheerful red cap. Helen sat opposite. She had great blue smudges under her eyes, and was as withdrawn and still as someone experiencing pain.

'It's not right,' thought Frances. 'She shouldn't look like that. I've never seen her look happy since I moved in here. No one does in this house. She ought to be allowed to go out and meet other kids. They all should.'

She thought of the long evening ahead with its study hours and the token exercise run which had never lost its nightmare quality. She saw that evening multiplied, over and over, until she was grown up and had, presumably, learned to accept this way of life without question. And after the war, was life going to be the same as now, with everything prescribed and strict and nobody allowed to have any fun?

In her restlessness, her chair scraped on the floor, and Mr Tyrell frowned at the noise. Aunt Loris silently gathered the empty dessert bowls and poured tea, and in total silence each person at the table took a cup.

'I can't bear this any longer,' Frances thought.

'Finish your tea and stop fidgeting,' Mr Tyrell said to her. His eyes were never still. They ranged incessantly around the people at the table, as though he perhaps even drew enjoyment from holding such absolute power over the household.

'I can't stand it here,' Frances thought, quite calmly. 'I'm going to have to tell him so. I'll belong to the temple, if that's what they want, but I've just got to get away from the house for a few hours each day.'

She waited till the meal was finished and pushed the cotton-wool plug free with her tongue. Determination overcame squeamishness, and she spat the cotton wool out into her handkerchief and put it away in her pocket so she could talk. 'I want to go back to school,' she said in a voice that trembled in spite of the determination.

'What do you mean by that, Frances?' her aunt demanded. 'All the education you need is available right here in this house.'

'I want to be in a proper school with other kids.'

Mr Tyrell was watching her with no expression at all on his face. Frances ploughed solidly on. 'I just don't like being locked up all the time. It's getting on my nerves. I'm willing to keep on learning about the temple, and I don't want to be outside when the war comes. But it's too hard, living here like Rosgrana and Helen and Claire and giving up school and everything.'

'I told you she wasn't fitting in here,' Claire said. 'She never will.'

'All this is just because she's upset after the dentist,' Aunt Loris protested. 'She'll be all right in the morning, won't you, Frances? You tell your uncle that you don't really mean any of that about going back to school.'

'She means it,' Claire said. 'She sneers at everything we do. She thinks we're all a joke. And I've seen her yawning and not paying attention when the video tapes are being shown. That's why she can't answer the questions correctly afterwards.'

'I don't sneer,' said Frances. 'I'd never make fun of anyone's religion.'

'It's your religion now,' said Mr Tyrell. 'I don't see how you can possibly have any doubts, after all our careful teaching. It's quite out of the question for you to attend school. I can't allow you to be corrupted any further by people who have no connection with the temple. And I won't allow you to place this house in jeopardy by living a life apart from us, even if it's only for a few hours each day.'

'It would be all right,' Frances pleaded. 'I would give them a different name, like we did today at the dentist. And I'd never tell anyone about here. I wouldn't let them walk home with me or know where I lived. Can't you see I'm not used to living like this? I'll go crazy if I can't get out for a few hours each day.'

'You have no choice in the matter. For your own salvation, it's necessary that you be brought up here with my girls and live as they do. It's the temple rule.'

Frances suddenly hated his authoritative voice.

She hated all the Tyrells, their quiet voices and disciplined, joyless manners. Everywhere, from every corner of the table, she met their critical eyes, appraising her, censoring her. Except Helen, who did not meet her eyes at all.

Last of all, she looked at Mr Tyrell's clean pale hands folded so neatly on the tablecloth. She stared at the hands and thought of them crushing the life from a small helpless bird. She felt sickened.

'What if . . . what if I prefer to live somewhere else?' she whispered.

'It's not possible. Not now.'

'You can't keep me here if I don't want to stay.'

'Yes, I can,' said Mr Tyrell, as calmly as though he were just rebuking her for table manners. 'There is no way out of this house unless I permit it.'

Frances burst into tears. 'I'll run off, then!' she cried. 'The first chance I get! I just wish I'd told that dentist who I really was, then you would have looked stupid giving him that false name. You couldn't have done anything, if I'd told that dentist. You would have to let me stay there, outside.'

Through the scalding tears she saw her aunt's shocked face, and Rosgrana and Claire watching her with their strange, veiled eyes that told nothing at all. 'All those people we saw on the way home have got just as much right as you have to live!' she raged. 'You're not any better than them just because you belong to the temple. I don't think I even believe in that war, anyhow. I was just scared . . . you all went on and on about it, and I got frightened. If it doesn't happen, just think about the waste . . . all those years cooped up here in this house and for nothing! I don't want to have that happen to me. I won't let it!'

She felt bereft of all dignity, crying at the table into their adamant, controlled slence. Nobody came to comfort her. Even Helen was looking at her oddly. They rose and went into the sitting room for the study time, and she was left in the kitchen with Aunt Loris. Frances finished her wild crying. She felt drained, enervated, with nothing to show for that outburst. Aunt Loris began to clear the table and do the washing up. 'She's giving me time to stop blubbing and get myself together,' Frances thought. 'Then she'll be like she used to be. She'll stick up for me and ring Kerry's place and let me go and stay there tonight.'

But when her aunt turned around, her face was rigid with an enormous, terrifying anger. 'How could you!' she said viciously. 'How dare you! You know what this place means to me, and you went and tried to spoil it! I've never felt so ashamed! You're not even my child, but I still brought you here with me because I wanted you to be saved, too. And you're too stupid to be taught. Just when I thought the hard part of my life was over, and something worthwhile starting, you go and try to ruin it!'

'I wasn't doing anything of the sort,' Frances

protested. 'All I wanted was for him to let me go back to school. The rest just happened. I didn't mean to say all that about the war. You can't even talk to him and ask him things. He just won't listen properly. Couldn't I board with Kerry's Mum and Dad? It'd be much better if I went away and lived somewhere else for awhile. Till I got myself all sorted out. Can't you make him let me do that?'

'I wouldn't dream of questioning any decision Finley made,' Aunt Loris said stiffly. 'And I'll tell you one thing, my girl. If you go on arguing and making mistakes and causing trouble, you certainly will be sent away to live somewhere else. They won't let you live alongside everyone else in a decent temple household. They can't take the risk of the blight spreading to others just because of one weak person. But you won't be sent back out there, either. They never let people go outside to live, when they're too weak to live by the rules. First you'd be sent to the temple to stay while they did their best to make you see your mistakes, but if they decided that you're too stubborn to be taught, then . . .'

'Then what?' Frances asked, frightened.

'Then you'd be sent to a special place they have for people who can't be taught. Way out in the country somewhere, where there aren't any other houses around, or towns or anything. There's no way of getting out of that place, once you land up there. It's got to be like that. We can't have people spreading a lot of lies about us, to everyone else in the world who doesn't belong to the temple. If you fail, you won't be allowed to drag us all down with you. They'd send you off to that place, and your name would be taken off the temple lists, and it would be as though you never existed anywhere.'

'How do you know there's a place like that?'

'From meetings at the temple. While you were out having your tooth seen to, Rosgrana was telling me they had to send a boy there. The girls heard about it while they were at their meeting. One of the boys who worked at the temple market garden, but he wasn't even grateful for that privilege. He started questioning the way of things. They had him brought back to the temple for a while, but he still thought he knew better than those appointed by God. You can ask Rosgrana if you think I'm just making it up to scare you into being good. Ask Helen. It hit home to her, I can tell you. She was white as a sheet when Rosgrana was telling me about it. So you'd better think seriously, Frances, because it could happen to you if you don't shape up. Finley's been very patient with you, and everyone's made allowances, but we certainly can't have this household disrupted just because you find things a bit hard. I value my salvation and the salvation of Finley and his family more than anything else. Salvation is what matters. If you get into trouble with the council, you can't expect me to show you any mercy. You understand?'

Frances nodded slowly, understanding one thing only, that her aunt's face had become the face of a total stranger.

Twelve

She was no longer allowed to go out with the others each evening for exercise. 'Until I'm satisfied that you've had a change of attitude,' Mr Tyrell said. 'It's too much responsibility for whoever goes with you. I'm doing this for your own good, Frances.'

Frances sank once more into the stultifying routine of the household, aware of time passing only because of the calendar in the kitchen where Rosgrana erased each day with a pencil. She drifted in and out of the days, so alarmed by what her aunt had told her, that she became outwardly as quiet and obedient as Claire. Her life, before Aunt Loris's marriage, seemed no more substantial than a half-remembered dream. Sometimes she tried to recall the faces of people from that time, but it seemed to her that she had been living for ever in that secluded house. And the only faces she had ever known were those of the Tyrells, and her aunt, who was herself a Tyrell now by name and choosing.

The only real companionship she had was that of the stray cat. In the long afternoons, which Claire spent downstairs, Frances would move the table on the landing forward and open the little lattice window. She would call softly and wait, and very often the cat would appear and she would bribe it to stay with food stolen from the kitchen.

The cat grew accustomed to her being there at certain times. It knew that the open window meant food and refuge from the bleak winter weather. Frances realized that there was a risk involved. At any time Claire might come upstairs, or Rosgrana to fetch sewing materials. Aunt Loris and Mr Tyrell rarely came upstairs at all. She wasn't concerned about Helen, who had lately grown quiet and morose. She had withdrawn into a melancholy world of her own and spent the afternoons in her room with the door shut.

The cat enabled Frances to endure the long tedious hours that weren't filled with housework. First she would feed it with whatever she had managed to take from the kitchen, and then she sat on her bed and held it lovingly in her arms. She couldn't understand why the council forbade such clean, beautiful animals, and considered taking it downstairs to show the girls how lovely it was. Surely Rosgrana and Claire would be as captivated as she was, and welcome the idea of having it live there officially. But then she would remember what Mr Tyrell had done to the bird, and shuddered.

It was Claire who found out about the cat. She stood in the doorway of the attic, staring, and her face looked queer and shocked.

'It was hungry,' Frances said appeasingly. 'I don't think anyone owns it. Why are you gawking at me like that? It's only a cat, for goodness sake.'

'Only?' Claire demanded shrilly. 'How dare you bring it into my room? Cats carry diseases, everyone knows that!'

'This one keeps itself clean and it hasn't even got fleas; I checked.' Frances hoisted up the cat and carried it to her, confident that its beauty would beguile her into a softened attitude. But Claire fended her off with flailing, panicky hands. 'What's up with you?' Frances asked, puzzled. 'Are you scared of cats? This one won't hurt you, honest. It's a quiet little thing. Go on, give it a pat. I'll hold it tight while you pat it, and you'll see there's nothing to be scared of.'

'No! Don't you dare bring it near me! I'm going to tell Father about your letting that thing inside when it's not allowed. You're an awful girl! Doing a wicked thing like that and breaking the rules!'

'What's so bad about it? The rules are bad, that's what! They don't make any sense.'

'You don't understand about the rules. We've all tried to teach you and you've failed. They'll probably make you go and stay at the temple and learn there. And I shan't be sorry to see you go, either!'

'No one's sending me any place I don't want to go!' Frances hissed.

Helen came quickly out of her room, and assessed at once what was taking place on that battlefield.

'What's all the noise about, girls?' Aunt Loris called from the bottom of the stairs. 'Is anything the matter?'

'It's all right,' Helen said, going to the banisters. 'It was just a big spider on the ceiling. There's no need for you to come up. Claire was frightened, but it's all right now. I dealt with it.' She came up to the attic and put her arms around Claire and rocked her gently like a mother soothing a distraught child. Claire's wild expression slowly faded to petulance.

'She brought that animal in here and fed it,' she said querulously. 'In the room I have to sleep in. And it's against the rules, everyone knows. She must have known, too, but she went ahead and did it, anyhow.'

Frances longed to put the cat outside, into safety, but didn't want to draw Claire's attention to the little window hidden behind the table. She wanted to keep it a secret, if possible.

'Claire, you'd better calm down, now,' Helen said. 'It's very silly, getting yourself into such a state. And if you tell Father, I'll be the one who gets into trouble. The cat must have followed me inside, when I came in from the back yard. I must have left the screen door open. There's no other way it could have got in here.' Her eyes signalled urgency over Claire's head. 'Frances, shut the cat in my room for the moment, and I'll take it back outside myself when I go down.'

Frances retreated into Helen's room with the cat cradled protectively in her arms, and after a while Helen came in and shut the door. 'Is she going to tell your Dad?' Frances said sulkily.

'I don't think she will. I managed to calm her. She's afraid of animals and that's why she became so hysterical. I suppose it's because she never sees any. I kept telling her it was my fault and that I left the back door open. And it is really my fault. I've been feeding that cat, too, for a long time, even before you came here to live. I used to let it in through the little window after everyone was asleep. But I haven't done it for weeks, because I realized it was wrong.'

'There's nothing wrong about it. If you asked your father nicely, isn't there a chance he'd let us keep it?'

'I can't ask him! If he found out, there'd be terrible trouble. I hate rows. It's easier to give in, for the sake of peace. They'd think very badly of me if they found out I was leading someone your age into disobedience. Rosgrana would never do anything like that. You'll just have to put the cat outside, it's safe to use the little window now that Claire's gone downstairs, but you must never

147

open that window again. I shouldn't have touched it, either. The table's always been in front and Father overlooked it when he was wiring all the others. I should have told him that there was a window that wasn't safe. The house is everyone's responsibility. The whole house is supposed to be safe.'

'Why didn't you tell him?' Frances asked curiously.

'It was just something that belonged to me. It seemed nice, no one else knowing about it. I used to come upstairs when everyone else was busy, and look out into the middle of the vines. A bird built its nest just outside, one year. Tiny blue eggs, no bigger than a thimble . . . I knew it was wrong, all the time I was doing it. But I couldn't bear to have that window nailed up like the others.'

'You're not the only person who gets sick of closed up windows. I do.'

'It's different for you. They make allowances, because you have those other things to unlearn. Even with your outburst in the kitchen, they think you can still be taught. But they expect me to be strong all the time, like Rosgrana. There's no room for weak people. If you're weak you get sent away. Like Paul, my friend I was telling you about, that time I was drying my hair. Paul couldn't stand the strict life any more, and started to question things. And now he's . . . they've sent him away . . .' She turned aside and pretended to be tidying the top of her bedside table, but Frances could tell that she was close to tears.

'Don't,' Frances said. 'Please don't cry. They can't make him stay at that place where they've got him, not for ever. He'll come back and see you.'

'They send them away for ever,' Helen said tiredly. 'Didn't your aunt explain it to you? Paul had counselling at the temple, and I begged and begged him to co-operate with them, but he wouldn't listen. So they've sent him away.'

'Aunt Loris tried to scare me about that place. Listen, I bet that Paul will find a way out. He'll just sneak off when they're not looking, same as I'd do if they ever sent me there.'

'They'll take care that he doesn't, because of the danger to the rest of us. Once you've been to the temple and know where it is, they never let you get away. The temple's sacred. All the files and documents are kept there. It's the heart of the whole thing. We're warned over and over at the meetings what happens to weak people.'

'They can't treat people like that! That temple's a terrible thing to belong to.'

'It's the only thing to belong to. What else is there? The war . . .'

'What if that war doesn't ever come?'

'Nothing can stop it. And all those people out there are going to die.'

'But they haven't done anything! It's nice out there. Don't you ever want to go out and see for yourself and make up your own mind?'

'Of course not. I wouldn't break the temple rules.'

'But you already did,' Frances said triumphantly. 'You kept the little window secret so you could look out.'

'That was just foolishness. And I'm never going to do anything like that again. Listen, the names that Father chose for us all mean "light". You can look them up. There's a book down in the big room about names and what they mean. Father chose ours, because when the war is over, we'll be the ones saved, the only ones, and there's nothing that can make me risk that.'

'That's only what the people at the temple tell you. What if they're wrong? You ever thought of that? That you're stuck here for nothing? That's what your life will be if they're wrong, a great big nothing! And I'd have thought if you're so rapt in that Paul whatever his name is, you'd want to get out and tell the police and have him rescued from that prison place. That's probably what he's thinking. He's probably waiting, hoping every day you'll come along and get him out!'

'I'm not going to listen to you any more!' Helen cried. 'Leave my room! qnd I'm not going to help you out of any mistakes, either, or have anything to do with you until you start thinking the way we all do. Claire's right, and it was an error letting you come here to live with us. I can tell what's going to happen to you. You'll finish in that place where they sent Paul.'

'No, I won't,' said Frances. 'You want to know what my name means? It means "free". I looked it up in that book when we were cleaning out the big room. And I thought then what a dumb name for me to have, when I'm not free at all in this house. No one is. So that's why I'm getting out of it, first chance I get. And if you really like Paul, you'll come with me.'

She carried the cat out to the landing and pushed it gently through the little window. The cat stretched and leaped away into the tangle of vines. Frances couldn't see where it had gone. The window was too small to be of any use for that. It was small and totally useless, an incongruous decoration in that grim house.

Thirteen

Claire became ill. Each evening, when the darkness settled around the house, she coughed in long wracking spasms. Rosgrana gave her medicine from the storeroom and kept her in bed, and her hands on the coverlet were as still and fragile as flowers.

'Why don't you call the doctor when she's coughing like that?' Frances asked.

'It's just bronchitis. She gets it every winter. And we don't have anything to do with doctors. All they do is prescribe terrible chemicals and drugs.'

'But I was allowed to go to the dentist. What's the difference between that and Claire?'

'Claire's illness will run a natural course,' Rosgrana said testily. 'It's not the same at all as a broken tooth. You're only a child, and you argue and argue. I'm tired of it, Frances. I've never had to put up with it from Helen and Claire, even when they were much smaller than you. This winter has been the worst I can remember, with you underfoot all the time, always arguing and thinking that you know better than we do how to manage things!'

'A doctor would give her some antibiotics and she'd start getting better straight away. I got bronchitis once, and that's what happened to me. Aunt Loris took me to the doctor in Scully Road. They had this terrific big aquarium in the waiting room, covering a whole wall nearly. You don't mind waiting when you've got something like that to look at. And I didn't have to have a shot of penicillin or anything, just capsules, and they started to work in a couple of days.'

'Father doesn't want you talking to us about what you did out there. And I certainly have no wish to listen. None of us have. All that has nothing whatever to do with us.' Rosgrana marched out of the room with Claire's lunch tray, and Frances sighed and looked in the wardrobe for the pullover she'd come upstairs for. She longed suddenly for brighter clothes, something red, something decorated with pom poms or embroidery. Everything in the wardrobe looked sombre and depressing, like the room itself. She felt sorry for Claire, having to stay in bed in such dismal surroundings.

'Would you like me to bring up any more of your books?' she asked.

'Rosgrana is looking after me.'

'Do you want me to stay here with you for a bit of company, then?'

'I don't want you up here at all,' Claire said. 'I've never been as sick as this before. I wouldn't be surprised if you brought this illness into our house.'

'That's rubbish!' Frances cried, forgetting how ill and pathetic Claire looked. 'Of all the stupid things to say! I never had a cold or anything when I came, and I've been here for three months. You couldn't possibly have caught anything from me!'

'Then it must be because of that cat you had in the room. Everyone knows cats spread disease.'

'Thousands of houses have cats for pets, and those people don't get sick. Cats are perfectly clean. It wouldn't do this house any harm at all, having an animal around for a pet. Might make it a nicer place to live in, that's for sure.'

'You won't be in it for much longer, anyhow,' Claire said.

'What do you mean by that?'

'The day after tomorrow, they're sending you to the temple to live for a while. So you'll be away from everyone until you stop fighting and arguing. Father and Rosgrana were discussing it.'

Claire drew the blankets up to her chin and shut her eyes, and the rejection was like a blow in the face. Frances stood staring at her for a moment, and then ran downstairs to find her aunt. Aunt Loris, who had looked after her all those years. Who would look after her now?

Aunt Loris was tidying the shelves in the pantry, methodically scrubbing each one with scouring powder. Frances thought, through her panic, that she scarcely ever saw her aunt just sitting down and relaxing these days. Aunt Loris toiled in the house compulsively, as though she were in bondage to it. Even now, when Frances burst into the kitchen, she didn't stop work, but continued scrubbing non-existent dirt from the spotless shelves. 'What is it, Frances?' she asked, annoyed. 'You're not to charge around the house like that. Even if Finley's out, one of the girls could mention to him that you've been running about and making a noise. You never seem to learn.'

'Claire said just now . . . she said they were going to make me go and stay at the temple. To live there. She said it had all been fixed.'

'There's no need to carry on like that about it, child. At the temple they'll be able to spend a lot of time with you and make certain you're properly instructed. Finley thought we could do it here, but it hasn't worked out that way at all. They've been too strong, those bad influences from you going to school, and going to movies and picking up all those ways out there. You're resisting all the teachings, Frances. We're seriously troubled by it.'

'I can't believe in something just by reading a lot of words and listening to a lot of boring lectures on video! I couldn't even understand half of them.'

'But you've had much more than that. You've

had the girls as an example since you've been here, and Finley's always been more than generous giving up his valuable time to go over and over those teachings with you. But you still keep asking why we won't let you go back to school. Things certainly can't go on as they are.'

'I won't go and live at that temple!'

'You haven't got any choice. I want this house kept peaceful and I don't want my husband worried all the time about the effect you're having on the girls.'

'That's all you think about,' Frances said bitterly. 'Him and those daughters of his and this house. What about me? I've got some rights, too, haven't I? I never asked to come to a place like this to live.'

Her aunt polished the shelf fussily with a dry cloth until the surface gleamed, then she began to replace the containers of food. 'All the time I've been talking,' Frances thought, 'all the time, she hasn't stopped what she's doing for one second, hasn't even looked at me.'

'I wish you hadn't brought me here, Aunt Loris,' she said. 'I wish you'd left me out there.'

Aunt Loris finally turned and looked at her. 'So do I, now,' she said. 'I see it's been a mistake. I honestly don't feel that you're numbered amongst the ones who are going to be saved from that war. If you had been, you'd have grown like Finley's girls by now. I really don't see you in that number, Frances.'

'How do you see me, then?' whispered Frances, but needed no spoken answer. Interloper, her aunt's eyes said. Intruder.

Starting on the ground floor, Frances made a systematic check of the windows. Like the ones in the attic, they had all been sealed by heavy nails driven in at points around the timber frames, and each one was wired to the alarm system. She considered smashing the laundry window and climbing out, but knew that they would come and stop her, because the alarm would be triggered. And it was pointless, anyhow, for there was no way out of the back yard. If she could get into the front garden somehow, she would be able to escape because of the unlocked front gate, purposely inconspicuous from its neighbours. The sitting room was out of the question, with its stout wooden shutters. Perhaps she could break one of the upstairs front windows and climb down before they reached her.

But even as she nerved herself to go upstairs and do this, she remembered coming back from an exercise run and glancing up at the front of the house. The windows there had been screened with heavy wire grilles, like the ones at the temple. She could remember the way the moonlight had glinted on them. There was no way out of the house.

Sick at heart, she slumped down on the last step in the hallway and thought of Kerry's house, and the warmth of ordinary people in an ordinary family. All her hopes and thoughts centred on Kerry's family. There was nowhere else. There was no other person in all that vast city who had any interest in her whatsoever. Mrs Wallace in the shop below the flat would have forgotten all about her now. It was a chilling thought, that nobody knew where she was, or cared; that there was no relative who would think, 'It's Frances's birthday soon. I must sent her a card. Let me see, what's her new address?' Frances realized with a jolt that she didn't know it herself. She didn't know the name of the suburb where this house was, or the street name, or the number of the house. She didn't even know who lived in the house next door.

The house next door!

Aunt Loris called for her to take some linen out to hang on the line. Rosgrana had to be fetched to unlock the kitchen door, and she did so impatiently, because she'd been on her way upstairs with a glass of orange juice for Claire. She didn't wait in the doorway to readmit Frances, but went on up to the attic.

It was the first time Frances had been outside by herself. She clipped the last peg into place, and keeping a cautious eye on the back of the house, went over to inspect the fence. There was no way to climb it. The toolshed, which perhaps held a ladder, was kept locked, and there was nothing else in the yard she could use as a substitute. She wouldn't be able to bring something from the house outside without being seen. And even if she could, she thought glumly, there was no way of climbing over the strands of barbed wire at the top.

She wondered about the house next door. Its roof wasn't visible above the fence. The people who lived there must think it peculiar, having a neighbour who fenced his property off with such a barricade. People in suburbs didn't put up high fences surmounted by barbed wire and an alarm system. How had Mr Tyrell managed to get away with that? Wasn't there some law that people had to share the cost of a fence put up to divide two properties? She couldn't understand how any neighbour would have agreed to such a massive, hideous-looking structure as that corrugated iron fence. She rapped on its surface and listened, willing someone to be there on the other side. She could call over to them, explain, and they'd come over somehow and get her out.

'Frances!' Aunt Loris called sharply from the back door. 'Come inside this minute!'

Frances trailed back.

'What were you doing over there by the fence?' Aunt Loris demanded. 'There's no reason for you to be over there.'

'I was thinking how ugly it looked,' Frances said. 'If it was my yard, I'd rip it down and put up something nice, a nice green hedge or better still, nothing at all.'

'That fence is there for a purpose, as you very

well know. And I don't want you loafing around just because your uncle is out. There's your clothes to be got ready for your stay at the temple. I don't know how long they'll want to keep you there, so you'd better pack all your things. I've put my suitcase out in the hall for you, and all your clothes have got to be clean and ironed. I don't want them finding anything to criticize on that score.'

'I won't go,' Frances said defiantly. 'No one can make me. It'll be even worse than here, people nagging at me to believe in things I don't want to. They can lecture at me till they're blue in the face, but I'll never believe it's right living like this.'

'You believed in it when we first came.'

'Only because I was scared, everyone talking about that war. And everyone getting jittery when the doorbell rang. It seemed real, all those provisions downstairs, it felt like being in a siege. But it doesn't seem real now. When he was driving me home from the dentist and I saw all these ordinary houses and ordinary people . . . it didn't make any sense . . .'

'It's not up to you to decide. You're too young.'

'I'm not too young to know that God wouldn't just pick out a group of people and kill off everyone else! Who'd want to believe in a god who carried on like a . . . like a teacher playing favourites! There wasn't anything bad about those people out there.'

'If you'd only let yourself be guided, you'd understand.'

'Guided by him?' Frances said savagely. 'By someone who'd crush a little bird in his hand? That's what he did once, Helen told me. He's the one needing to be guided, not me. I won't go to that temple.'

'Then there's only one other place left,' said her aunt.

Frances looked at her, engulfed by loss almost too great to bear. It was as though there had never been a time when the Tyrells were unknown to either of them. She remembered the hasty, slap-dash meals and the anxious budgeting in small flats. 'Aunt Loris . . .,' she pleaded, stretching out a hand, but her aunt took no notice. She had gone back to her housework.

Frances stood gazing at her for several minutes, then went out into the sad, empty hall. Her mouth set into a hard line. She went into Mr Tyrell's office and searched for the missing phone book. The filing cabinet and desk were still locked, and she had no tool to force them open. Names of people she could ring tumbled feverishly in and out of her mind; Kerry; Mrs Wallace who had owned the food shop below the flat; a teacher at school who had been specially kind; the receptionist at the dentist where Mr Tyrell had taken her. Useless names, paired with no magical code of numbers.

She knew that Mr Tyrell could come home at any moment. Or Rosgrana would soon be checking up on her. For such a large house, it was impossible to find any lasting privacy. There was no room that was not in use, no secret corner where she could really be by herself. If she loitered over a task, there was always someone sent to investigate and find out why she was so slow. She had very little time.

She picked up the receiver and dialled a wild combination of numbers and listened to a telephone ringing in some unknown place. It rang and rang, and nobody answered. She dialled another set of numbers, thinking crazily of little lottery balls, and again there was the brisk ringing of a phone in some strange room. Frances was about to replace the receiver when an annoyed voice, breathless, as though its owner had had to run in from outside, said tersely, 'Yes? Hello?'

'I can't find a phone book,' Frances gabbled. 'There's a girl called Kerry Hodges, could you please look up her number for me? She went to my school . . .'

'Don't give me that! All you kids think it's smart to play around with the phone when your parents are out.'

'Scully High School. And she was my best friend . . . There's no phone book and I don't want them to know I was trying to . . . oh, please, listen . . .'

'You can get into serious trouble for dialling people's numbers and mucking around. Just don't try it on again, that's all.'

There was an angry little thud on the other end of the line as the receiver was replaced, and silence. Frances heard Rosgrana calling her from the hall, but she stayed where she was. Her finger-tips desperately scrabbled numbers out of the dial, the receiver hummed strange signals, a tele-phone rang in someone else's house, but nobody came to answer it.

Helen called from the stairs, 'Frances isn't up here. She hasn't come upstairs at all. Perhaps she's in the big room. Or perhaps Father called her out-side. He just arrived home.'

When they finished searching the house for her, and Rosgrana finally opened the door to the office, Frances still continued to sit holding the telephone, listening to that far away, useless ring-ing. 'I don't care,' she said, registering Mr Tyrell's fury through a blur of tears. 'This didn't work, but sooner or later I'll find a way to get out of here.'

He was like an appalling child, she thought, angry because she'd touched his possessions, unable to bear being thwarted in any way. And Aunt Loris was nervously trying to appease him, looking over his shoulder at Frances as though she had committed some terrible crime, as though she were a dangerous animal.

'He's the dangerous animal, not me!' Frances

said scornfully, and collected a great slap across the face that sent her reeling halfway across the room.

'Don't hit her, Finley,' Aunt Loris said. 'She's not worth wasting anger on. She doesn't know any better, and she'll be gone soon, anyhow, out of this house.'

'The sooner the better,' said Frances. She held the side of her face and walked upstairs, past Helen.

'It's not any better at the temple. It's worse,' Helen whispered, so bitterly that Frances spun around. But Helen was already walking downstairs, once again impassive and withdrawn, passing the still smouldering embers of that unpleasant scene as though none of it mattered very much, anyhow.

Fourteen

During the night the cat woke her by jumping up on her bed. It mewed a gentle query for food and Frances hushed it, but Claire didn't stir in her sleep. She looked frail and vulnerable, tucked into the neat bed, and the labour of her breathing alarmed Frances.

'They should get a doctor,' she thought, outraged. 'She's sick enough to go to a hospital.' She knew that Mr Tyrell would never allow that. Most likely Claire would be moved to the temple if her condition grew worse. And if she died at the temple, there would be nothing written down anywhere in the outside world to show that she had ever existed. No name in school registers, no face in school group photographs.

Frances, absently soothing the cat, got out of bed and looked down at Claire in the moonlight. Rosgrana had dosed her again with medicine from the storeroom. The medicine was in an old-fashioned-looking bottle which bore no pharmacy label, and Claire had fallen into a deep slumber after taking it. She was restive now, though, moving jerkily about in her sleep, and Frances found herself tensing each time she took a breath, waiting for the next rasping, painful inhalation.

The cat struggled in her arms, and she crept downstairs and got some food and fed it on the bathroom landing. While the cat ate hungrily, she lay flat on the floor and looked through the little window. She stuck an arm out with difficulty, and parted the thick vines, and found that she was looking straight down into the front yard. The window was too narrow to enable her to see more than a section of the bushes that screened the fence. She tried to remember, from the times she'd been allowed out at night to exercise, what was opposite the house. Everything had looked so strange and distorted in the dark. Was there a public telephone in that stretch of street, or a post-box? She couldn't even remember that.

'I could write a letter to Kerry,' she thought. 'And maybe talk Helen into slipping it in a letter-box, seeing they don't let me go running any more.'

She knew how futile that idea was, having seen how closely the girls stayed together on those exercise runs, like terrified sheep. Helen would never consent to do such a thing; and she didn't even know if there was a letterbox, and she had no stamp. Even if she did manage to get it into a letterbox, without a stamp it might end up in the dead-letter office. And that was exactly how she felt herself, like a small, forgotten letter, with no address, no postage paid, unclaimed and not wanted by anyone.

The cat finished its food and curled up and slept. Frances went downstairs again and got herself an apple and a glass of milk. In passing, she tried the kitchen door, knowing it to be a hopeless gesture, because Mr Tyrell always checked the formidable locks on both doors before he went to bed. If she couldn't get a letter into a postbox, perhaps she could somehow manage to throw one over the fence into the yard of the house next door. It needn't even be a letter to Kerry. Just a note, explaining what was happening in the house; whoever picked it up would surely tell someone in authority. And they'd come and stop Mr Tyrell from sending her to the temple, and make him fetch a doctor for Claire.

She went into the big room and closed the door so she could switch on the light. She found a sheet of paper and a pen and began to write. It was extraordinarily difficult to compose a letter to gain some unknown person's attention. She made several attempts and each sounded like a silly practical joke. She imagined a stranger reading what she'd written, and just crumpling up the paper and tossing it right down on the ground again. After perseverance and crossing out, she copied the result onto a fresh sheet. 'My name is Frances Parry and someone should do something about the people in the house where I live. It's the big one beside the alleyway. They belong to a church where they aren't allowed to go to school or out anywhere at all. He's broken the law. I want to get out of here and go back to school. There is also one of the girls who is very sick and I think she might have . . .' Frances didn't know how to spell pneumonia. 'I think she might die because they won't get a doctor. Please give this letter to Mrs Hodges; she's my best friend's mother and she'll know what to do. This isn't a joke, this letter. Everything in it is true.' She wrote down Kerry's address and read the note through anxiously, worried about her spelling and hand-writing. There was no envelope to put the letter in, but she folded it up and clipped it with a metal butterfly clip and put it in the pocket of her dressing gown.

Just as she was about to switch off the light, Claire began to scream. The thin wailing sound cascaded from the attic, and was brittle with panic. Frances's hand froze helplessly on the switch. She stood and listened to doors opening and footsteps hurrying up the stairs, and Claire's screaming slicing into the silence of the house.

Frances forced herself away from the light switch and up the stairs, huddling against the wall in her fear. Helen was standing in the doorway of her room. The screaming had stopped; Rosgrana and Aunt Loris were by Claire's bed, talking to her in soft, comforting voices.

Mr Tyrell came out of the attic room. He carried the cat by the fur around its neck and he passed the girls without a glance, without a word. Frances, numb with horror, saw that the cat was dead.

'There's nothing at all you can do about it,' Helen said tonelessly. 'I told you not to bring that poor cat into the house.'

Frances plunged up the stairs into the attic, calling out to her aunt. Her own voice, to her ears, sounded strange and babbling, as though it belonged to somebody else, far away, someone trapped and frightened and desperate. Someone should have stopped him doing such a thing, the voice was shrieking, over and over. Why hadn't they stopped him killing the cat? Someone should have stopped him.

'Who owns that voice?' she thought, quite calm and detached, listening. 'Who is it, shrieking in that terrible, terrible voice?'

The voice trailed away into whimpering and then silence. Nobody paid her any attention. They were involved with Claire, who had been sick all over the bed and the floor. They'd replaced the sheets with fresh ones, and her aunt was washing Claire's face and helping her into a clean nightgown. Claire's eyes glittered with fever, and she looked grey and pinched, like a very old person.

'How dare you bring a cat in here?' Aunt Loris said. 'Jumping up at her in the dark like that; she had no idea it was in the room. She said you had it in here once before, and she told you then, and you can't pretend you don't know it's against the temple rules. You just sneer at those rules, my girl, you just set yourself apart from us. I've given up on you.'

'She's sick,' Frances said, staring at Claire. 'It's not because she got a fright that she looks like that. She's really sick, and she needs a doctor.'

'You think it's as simple as that, that we can just get a doctor to make a house call here, or take the girl to a surgery for treatment? You saw the trouble he had, just getting you safely in and out of a dentist's without anyone finding out about us. You don't realize all the difficulties Finley goes through, trying to keep this house decent and true to the temple. All those enemies out there, like snipers in a jungle . . . We don't want you up here in Claire's room. She's not going to get any better with you around, that's obvious. You'd better take your mattress and blankets and sleep in Helen's room.'

Frances made herself move. She dragged the bedding down the little staircase and into Helen's room and crouched under the blankets like a small, frightened animal cowering in the roots of a tree. She tried to banish the memory of Mr Tyrell passing her on the stairs, his fingers clenched so terribly into the cat's fur, but the picture was etched into her mind as though set there by acid.

'Frances, are you warm enough?' Helen whispered out of the darkness. 'Do you need an extra rug?'

The coldness she felt had no connection with the makeshift bed. She shivered for a long time, contemplating repeatedly Mr Tyrell's hands, the lifeless body of the cat, the set of stairs. The pictures spun and whirled in front of her eyes as though she were witnessing him descend endless stairs after committing slaughter over and over again.

'He didn't have to kill it,' she said at last, when the shivering had ebbed enough to allow her to speak. 'It wasn't doing any harm. It wasn't the poor little cat's fault, Claire waking up in a fright. Why couldn't he just have put it out of the house?'

'If he'd done that, it would still be a temptation for you. You'd let it in, the next time you heard it calling out there. The temple rules . . . it's what we're taught . . . they're evil animals. There's not going to be a place for them after the war.'

'It makes me feel sick, what he did. And you all stood round and let him. I don't believe any of that nonsense, that you're all special and chosen and going to be saved. He's horrible, your father, a horrible cruel man.'

'He's in charge of the house . . .'

'You're not any more special than any of those people out there,' Frances said. 'What he's doing is wrong. It's terrible, all of you being kept locked in behind that fence.'

171

'It's not there to lock us in. It's there to keep everyone else out.'

'Then how come it needs a key to open it from the inside? You can't ever get out, unless your father opens the doors.'

'That doesn't matter. We've never wanted to go out.'

'Only because you've been brainwashed. You're scared, that's what.'

'We've got every reason to be! We know what it's going to be like, for all those people out there. I'm not going to listen to you anymore, Frances. It's dangerous listening to you. Father was saying before you came, that it would be good for us, seeing just what that kind of society could do to a person. That you'd be an example, and we could watch the process being reversed, evil into good. But you're like a hammer, battering away at everything that's important to us. I'm glad they're sending you to the temple. It's too hard, having you living in this house. Not for Rosgrana and Claire, because they're strong and they know anything you say is wrong and mustn't be heeded. I don't want to listen. Please be quiet!' Helen pulled the blanket over her head and rolled over to face the wall.

'As soon as I get out of this place,' Frances said. 'The first thing I'm going to do is find a beach and walk along it. That's something you've never done. It's beautiful, walking along a beach, even in winter. I don't suppose that Paul's ever seen the sea, either. If you came out with me, we could make them let Paul go. Lots of people would help us. You and Paul could go to the beach together. Any time you wanted. And there aren't any fences or locked doors or windows all painted over so you can't even look out.'

The weight of the darkness and silence in the room seemed almost tactile. She crawled out from her bedding and went to the window. Behind the curtains diffused light gleamed softly through the painted glass. She felt around on the table top and grabbed up the nail file and scraped at the paint. A gossamer-thin thread spiralled free. She scraped again and flakes of paint settled in a tiny snowstorm on the window sill.

'What are you doing?' Helen whispered. 'You must not go anywhere near the windows.'

Frances worked on stubbornly. The coating of paint was difficult to remove. She'd thought to scrape away huge sections so she could look out easily, but after five minutes work, there was just a cobweb of fine interlacing lines. The pressure of the nail file bit into her hand. She wrapped the hem of her nightgown around its handle and continued gouging out lines, working at a furious, urgent pace.

She bent and put an eye to the network of cracks, and tried to look out into the night, but the lines were too thin. There was nothing to be seen out there except a nebulous blur that could have been sky or buildings or foliage or anything at all.

'They'll think it was me,' Helen said wretchedly. 'They'll see the marks and think I made them and I'll get into trouble.'

'They won't think that,' Frances said with scorn. 'You're too much of a coward. You'd be too scared to make a space to look out.'

'I am not a coward,' said Helen. 'I did take off some paint once, so that I could look through.'

Frances's hand was raw from the file and the painful effort that had produced nothing more than a smudged glimpse of freedom. She returned to the mattress on the floor, but was unable to sleep. Occasionally there was a faint swish of tyres as a car passed in the street; the dog barked in its distant yard. The filtered light behind the window took on a fragile, warmer glow, and she heard the first early train. Someone walked by in the street whistling. They were all ordinary early morning sounds, and it was hard to believe that she was lying on the floor of a prison.

She looked across the room at Helen, knowing instinctively that she, too, had been lying awake for hours. 'Why would you want to look out a window?' Frances asked bitterly. 'You reckon you have everything you possibly need in this house. Why did you make a gap, then? So you could look out there and gloat over all those people you think are going to be knocked off in the war?'

'I didn't . . . It wasn't for anything like that. It was for . . .'

'What?' demanded Frances.

'To look at the stars.'

Fifteen

Claire was in obvious pain and her eyes were set in large dark rings. In spite of the chill in the room, her nightgown was damp with sweat. She moved her head fretfully on the pillows and peered at Frances, and through her, seeing nothing. Frances, nudged by fear, backed away and fled to the kitchen. 'Claire's looking terrible!' she cried. 'She's breathing funny and you've got to get a doctor for her.'

'Stop raising your voice like that,' Rosgrana said angrily.

'I should have thought you'd be the one yelling, making him do something to help her. She's your sister. She's never going to get better, just lying up there.'

'The arrangements of this house have nothing to do with you,' Rosgrana said. 'And if you can't behave and speak quietly, you're going to have to stay down in the storeroom until they come to get you tomorrow.'

'It wouldn't matter which room I was in,'

Frances said. 'What's so different about the rest of the house, anyway? It's all part of the same prison.' Her fingers closed upon the letter which she had transferred to her dress pocket. Her expression changed from belligerence to cunning. She would throw the letter over the fence and the people next door would come and attend to the appalling nightmare that was the Tyrells' way of life. Tonight she would be sleeping at Kerry's house. 'Do you want those sheets hung up on the line?' she asked.

'Yes. You'd be better employed offering help with the work than in being impertinent,' Rosgrana said coldly, and unlocked the back door.

Frances carried out the laundry basket. She carefully pegged up two sheets and using them as a screen, ran to the fence and tossed the weighted letter over. She heard the soft thud of its landing and hurried back to the clothesline. Struggling with another wet, heavy sheet, she glanced up at the window belonging to Helen's bedroom, and thought of the scratch lines. If she scraped away enough of the paint, she'd be able to look down into the yard next door and watch those people find her letter.

'It shouldn't have taken so long to hang up a few sheets,' Rosgrana scolded, letting her in and relocking the door. 'They won't tolerate that sort of laziness when you're living at the temple. Nobody will make allowances for you there. If you want to be accepted and come back here to live, you're going to have to alter your ways.'

'I don't want to be accepted,' Frances said. She looked at the packed suitcase, standing in readiness at the foot of the stairs. When the people next door found her letter and came in to take her away, she would leave it where it was. It was packed with all those neat, sad-coloured clothes. At Kerry's, she would borrow a pair of jeans and go for a walk somewhere, where she could yell and laugh and make as much noise as she liked.

She ran upstairs to Helen's room. Helen had stacked some books in front of the window, to conceal the scratched paint. Frances shoved them aside and began to enlarge the scratches. 'Those people could be reading the letter right now,' she thought. 'They'll come and ring at the door, and this time Rosgrana won't be able to get away with pretending there's no one home. Those people will break the door down if they have to.'

She scraped away flakes of paint into a coin-sized hole, large enough to look out and see where her letter lay, waiting to be picked up. 'You're not to touch that window again!' Helen said from the doorway. 'I covered it up so they wouldn't find out. Rosgrana is going to be watching what you do every minute until they take you to the temple tomorrow morning. They know you can't be trusted.'

'I won't be going to the temple,' Frances said triumphantly. 'I fixed it so I wouldn't have to.'

She bent and looked through the hole in the paintwork. There was a clear view over the fence into the property next door. She could see quite plainly where her message lay, like a bright arrowhead, on a patch of grass on the other side of the tall fence. Her aim had been true, and the message hadn't been snared up in bushes where nobody could find it. It was there in full view, just waiting for someone to come and pick it up.

And it was quite apparent that nobody would come. Ever. There was no house set in a garden next door, no neighbours. She looked down into a vacant block choked with blackberries and old dumped cars and ancient rubbish. Her letter lay in a little clearing in the middle of undergrowth so dense and thick that it was quite obvious that nobody had walked in there for a long time. The Tyrell house stood all by itself, quite alone, set in the framework of the street, the back lane, the alleyway, and the rubbish-strewn vacant block. And that was what her message was now, rubbish consigned to a dumping ground.

'I could have spared you the trouble of making that hole,' Helen said. 'I could have told you there was nothing to look at from this window. That block of land has always been like that.'

Frances couldn't answer, grieving for Kerry and a world where the sun gilded the surface of an ocean. She mourned for her aunt, who had locked them both into this barren life. And for Helen, who had never walked along a beach.

'Don't look like that,' pleaded Helen. 'Just be well behaved at the temple and don't argue with them, and do as they say. They might let me see you, when we come there for meetings. It's for your own good, Frances. I want you to be safe when the war comes, being one of us.'

Claire was whimpering from the little room at the top of the stairs. 'I must go back to her,' Helen said helplessly. 'They told me I have to sit with her. She's so ill that Father arranged for someone to come and examine her this afternoon. I have to stay with her until he comes.'

Frances kept her face turned away so Helen couldn't decipher the sudden rush of renewed hope. It didn't matter at all that there was nobody to come along and find that message; she was going to get out of the house anyway. She would walk out of that house with the doctor who was coming to look at Claire. Escape would be as easy as that.

Aunt Loris called her downstairs to help in the kitchen and she made plans behind a carefully sustained expression that showed nothing at all. 'I'll wait until the doctor's finished looking at Claire,' she thought. 'I'll wait on the stairs, and when he comes down I'll tell him everything about this house and the temple. And he'll listen and take me out of here.'

She grew jittery from waiting for the sound of the doorbell. The nervousness made her stupid and she spilled and dropped things. Her aunt grew more and more terse with her. 'I'll be thankful when tomorrow comes and you're off our hands,' she said angrily.

The doctor didn't arrive until late afternoon, and Mr Tyrell had to turn on the light in the hall to unlock the front door. Frances watched through the door of the laundry, where she'd been sent to sort out the ironing. The doctor went straight upstairs with Mr Tyrell, and Frances crept after them. Outside Helen's room, where the angle of the stairs made it impossible for two people to pass by each other. That would be the perfect place to hold the doctor's attention, when he came from seeing Claire. And he'd have to stand there and listen until she finished. It wasn't like a telephone, where the person on the other end could hang up on her unlikely story.

She waited just inside Helen's room, her eyes fastened on the closed door of the attic. 'You're not to go up there and disturb them,' Helen said quickly, looking up from her book.

'I wasn't going to,' Frances said. She remembered the times during the past months when Helen had been the only person in that house who had shown anything that resembled friendliness. She wished suddenly that her departure needn't be in such a manner. As soon as she confronted the doctor, the Tyrells' careful, secret way of life would come tumbling down like a card castle. And the pity of it was that they had assembled the cards with as much trust and labour as though they were paving stones.

She could hear the doctor's low voice behind the closed door, murmuring on and on, with nobody interrupting him or asking him questions. 'That doctor talks a lot,' she said impatiently. 'He shouldn't, when Claire's so sick. Sick people don't want to listen to anyone nattering at them.'

'Mr Hertes knows what he's about,' Helen said. 'He cured Rosgrana's migraine headaches once. We usually see him at the temple when we're sick, but Claire's too ill to be moved. That's why he's come to the house instead. He's not a doctor. He's a spiritual healer and a member of the temple council.'

Frances kept her eyes on the door of the attic and slowly counted to fifty while she battled away despair. In her mind she saw immense dark clouds creeping across a night sky, blotting out each star from horizon to horizon.

'Father wouldn't allow an ordinary doctor to come inside this house. We don't have anything to do with them. We always see Mr Hertes. Claire's never been as ill as this; none of us ever have. They think it might be caused by your being here; that you've destroyed the harmony, and Claire will start to get better once you've gone.'

'That's rubbish!' Frances cried. 'Illness isn't caused like that at all! Not the sort Claire's got, coughing and having a fever . . . I didn't have anything to do with it!'

'I tried to tell them so. Claire and Rosgrana kept saying that they couldn't concentrate anymore, with you living in the house, how distracting it was. Father was so worried that all our teaching would be affected. Frances, I'm so sorry that I couldn't do anything to change the way they felt. I tried to . . .'

The attic door opened and Mr Tyrell and the man came down the stairs. Frances shrank back out of sight, alarmed enough to think that she might be whisked out of the house that minute and taken away to live at the temple. There wasn't anything particularly frightening about Mr Hertes. She'd imagined that a member of the temple council would be quite different from anyone else, and show physical evidence of possessing strange and terrible powers. But Mr Hertes wasn't remarkable in any way. He was just a short middle-aged man with receding hair. He'd combed strands across in an effort to minimize the baldness. It was ludicrous to be afraid of anyone so ordinary. Frances tiptoed to the head of the stairs after they passed and looked down.

Mr Tyrell had unlocked the front door and its screen and was helping Mr Hertes on with his coat. Mr Hertes turned to put his arms into the sleeves and noticed Frances. 'Ah, the little girl who has been having difficulties,' he said. He beckoned her to come down into the hall, and held out his hand for her to shake. Frances took it unwillingly, disliking the way he stared at her.

'It's a very great pity that things have turned out in such a disappointing way,' he said. 'Someone of your age should allow themselves to be guided. You've caused everyone a lot of worry.'

Frances looked along the hall at Aunt Loris, hoping for an ally, but her aunt seemed only too eager to agree. 'Frances has been a thorough disappointment,' she said righteously. 'Everyone here has shown her the proper way to do things, and she wouldn't listen. She just wants no part of it. It's very sad, my own niece, and not being able to reach her, or get her to see the truth.'

'We thought from the first that she might need more intensive training than you people could give her in this house,' Mr Hertes said. 'But I'm sure she'll learn quickly during her stay at the temple. She'll eventually become just as much a child of light as Claire or Helen or Rosgrana. What do you think, Frances?'

Frances abruptly tore her hand loose from his. She ducked under his arm through the unlocked door and ran. She wrenched open the gate and fled into the dusk, where the street lamps spilled great bronze pools amongst the shadows. She ran diagonally across the street towards the nearest house with light showing. The softly glowing amber squares of windows promised people, ordinary rational people who would take her in out of the darkness. She sped up a pathway and banged hysterically at the door.

Turning her head, she saw Mr Tyrell and her

aunt had come out onto the pavement and were standing under the street lamp. Mr Tyrell was preparing to cross the road, not running in frenzied desperation as she had done. He stood under the street lamp and looked calmly in both directions to check for traffic.

Frances pounded on the door. There were slow footsteps on the other side, and a woman opened it and looked out at her.

'Listen . . . there's a sick girl . . . they won't let me out . . .'

The woman had a rounded dreamy face and slow ways. She took off her glasses and rubbed them on her apron and peered at Frances huddled on her doorstep. 'What is it?' she asked. 'I can't understand you, dear, what you're saying . . .'

'I want to go back to school and they won't let me,' Frances cried, shaken into tears. 'I want Kerry . . . They never let me out . . . I never . . .' Her half sentences winged into the darkness like frightened birds.

Mr Tyrell and her aunt had crossed the street. They walked sedately up the pathway of the house and the woman glanced at them over Frances's shoulder.

'Please . . .' sobbed Frances. 'I don't want to go back to that place! Can't you . . .'

'What is it you want, love?' the woman asked. Aunt Loris and Mr Tyrell stepped up on the porch, and Mr Tyrell put his arm around Frances and held her tight. 'I can't understand anything she's saying, babbling on like that,' said the woman. Mr Tyrell smiled at her with immense charm.

'I'm so sorry our little niece disturbed you,' he said. 'She's mentally handicapped. She's at a special school and becomes confused when she's in a strange house. We're looking after her for the night.'

'We left the front door open and she wandered off,' Aunt Loris said.

'Poor little Margaret,' Mr Tyrell said gently, stroking Frances's hair. 'There's no need to cry. We found you again. There's nothing to worry about.'

Their soft voices lapped at Frances, drowned her. 'Please . . .' she whispered. 'Please, they won't let me . . .'

'Sad, isn't it?' said the woman with easy sympathy. 'Poor little thing, she could have got hit by a car. Must be a handful for you to mind.' She looked at Frances uncertainly, her look a mixture of the embarrassment with which people regard handicapped people in public and a barely concealed thankfulness that she did not have to be personally involved.

Mr Tyrell's hand closed around Frances's arm, just above her elbow. The grip was strong enough to pull her away from the door and off the porch. 'Silly goose,' he said lightly. 'Giving your aunt and uncle such a fright, and bothering the neighbours.'

The woman stepped out onto her porch and watched Mr Tyrell walk Frances down the path to the gate. 'She's very upset, isn't she, poor little soul?' she said to Aunt Loris. 'We don't know our own blessings until we realize there are kiddies like that, needing that much care and attention.'

'I don't want to go back to that house!' Frances shrieked, hooking her free hand around the gate post and clinging.

'The special school she goes to is lovely and modern,' Aunt Loris told the woman. 'It's a sort of nursing home, where she boards. She gets into a state when her routine's interrupted. They've got a flu epidemic at that school and they're a bit short-staffed. That's why the matron rang and asked us to have her tonight. She'll settle down. Always does. Thank you for being so understanding about it. I suppose it gave you a turn, her banging on your front door like that. She's a bit spoiled, too, and a right little madam if she doesn't get her own way. But you mustn't let us keep you out in the cold like this any longer.'

Mr Tyrell unclamped Frances's hand from the gate post and picked her up easily and carried her across the road. She looked back at the house whose lighted windows had promised sanctuary. Its front door was closing now. Aunt Loris hurried across to join them and when she was inside the Tyrells' house, Mr Tyrell put Frances down and shut the door. 'There's no point crying,' he said.

'It was very selfish and foolish of you to run off like that, but there's no harm done.'

'I'll get out again tonight!' Frances said. 'I'll smash the windows and get out and make that woman over there listen to me.'

'Can't she go to the temple tonight, Mr Hertes?' Aunt Loris asked tiredly.

'The staff assigned to Frances won't be available until tomorrow morning. Meanwhile, you must take steps to see that she doesn't cause any more potentially dangerous situations for this house. Once she's at the temple, of course, the responsibility will be out of your hands. And quite a responsibility it's going to be. I hadn't realized the extent . . .'

'When I get out of here tonight, I'll tell them all about that temple!' Frances said. 'I'll tell the police where it is!'

Mr Hertes stared at her intently.

'I know where your precious temple is!' Frances cried. 'I followed Aunt Loris there the day she got married, and I'd know that crummy building anywhere. It's five streets up from a station called Bowan. It looks like a barracks or a prison or something, and I'm not going to live there! You can't shove people in there if they don't want to go, and that's why I'm going to get the police. They'll find all your files and everything . . .'

Her voice, racing after her thoughts, stopped abruptly. She could tell from Mr Hertes's face that a person who knew the whereabouts of the temple was in danger.

'Frances will change, after she's lived at the temple,' Helen said urgently. 'I know she will. It will be all right, Mr Hertes. Frances will accept the teachings.'

'She won't have any choice but to accept them,' said Mr Hertes. 'Not now.'

Sixteen

'You brought it upon yourself,' Rosgrana said. 'We can't take the risk of having you upstairs, not after all those things you said you'd do. You're going to have to spend the night down here. You can make as much fuss as you choose. Nobody will hear a sound.' She went up the stairs and bolted the door behind her.

It was cold in the basement, and the small electric radiator she had left gave scarcely more than a visual effect of heat. Frances yanked one of the blankets from the stretcher, which Rosgrana had made into an impeccably tidy bed, as though tidiness mattered. Nothing mattered now, Frances thought drearily. She hugged the blanket around her like a shell and slumped on the bed. In the morning, very early, she would be taken away from the house. She would be kept at the temple for three months and, at the end of that time, her situation would be reassessed by the council. Mr Hertes had explained that to her. She knew that three months of intensive training would do nothing to alter the way she felt. She had seen the confirmation of that in Helen's eyes, gazing at her with hopeless pity while Mr Hertes had been speaking.

'They'll soon find out it's no good and they'll send me to that other place,' Frances thought. 'That last place they have. And I'll never get out of there. I'm useless. I couldn't even manage to get away from this house.'

The taste of failure goaded her up the stairs to the little door. She battered it with her fists until the racket filled her head with pain, but no one came, even in anger. She prowled around the storeroom, although she knew from the hours spent tidying the shelves and storing away supplies of food that there were no windows. There was no way out except through the pantry door.

She was going to be taken away at six o'clock in the morning, when it would still be dark, with nobody about on the streets. She would be leaving the house as secretly as she had entered it. Even if she yelled and struggled in the van, there wouldn't be anyone to listen or to help her. Perhaps when Mr Tyrell came to get her tomorrow, she could pretend to be sick, as seriously ill as Claire. But the only thing she would gain from that pretence would be time spent upstairs in bed, until they found out she was lying. And she'd still be taken to the temple afterwards. It was useless to think that she could battle against the people of the temple with their fanatical faith which gave

190

them such strength and unity. The council was strong enough to cause whole families to shut out the wonder and magic of the world. She had no weapons to use against strength like that. She began to imagine what her life would be like at the temple and afterwards, and the prospect was so chilling that she crept back to the tenuous shelter of the blanket.

The door opened and a shaft of light fell down the staircase like a waterfall. Helen came down the stairs. 'It's no use running up there and screaming,' she said. 'He told me to warn you about that at once. He's in the kitchen, and he'd just force you straight down here again. I've brought you something to eat.'

Frances didn't even look at the tray.

'Please eat something,' Helen pleaded. 'You'll be hungry during the night, and I shan't be allowed down here again to see if you're all right. I went to a lot of trouble. Rosgrana and your aunt said that you didn't deserve anything after running out into the street like that. I had to ask and ask before they gave in.'

'I don't want anything to eat,' Frances said. 'What I want is those keys. You've got to get them away from him when everyone's asleep. You know it's wrong, what they're doing. You've got to help me get away from this house.'

'You mustn't expect me to do anything like that. I wouldn't be able to go on living here afterwards. They'd never forgive me.'

'You don't have to stay. I know a place where we could go. You could come with me. Kerry's mother would look after us, and she wouldn't let him drag you back here, either, if you didn't want to. You won't want to, once you've seen what it's really like out there.'

'We've been told what it's like. I don't want any part of it.'

'You're just too scared to go out and see for yourself! All you do is listen to what they tell you and make a stupid little hole to look at the stars! Just a coward, that's all you are, living in a prison all your life and you never even try and get away! Go on, get back upstairs. I don't want you hanging around me. I don't want any of their food. I won't eat anything at the temple, either. I'll spend every minute there trying to get out.'

'You mustn't make the council angry. I don't want you to try to escape; it would be the end of everything. I'd lose you, too, just as I lost Paul.'

'If you got the keys for me . . .'

'I'd destroy my whole family. You can't ask me to do that.'

'Not destroy them,' said Frances. 'Free them. That's what you'd be doing, like letting birds out of a cage.' She gazed around the basement, scanning the provisions stored to keep the world at bay; food and clothing, and candles to supply light in the aftermath of a hypothetical war. 'If you don't get me the keys,' she said desperately, her eyes sharp with guile, 'I'll light a fire down here

192

after everyone's asleep. People in the street will smell the smoke and ring for the fire brigade.'

'You can't! You mustn't do such a thing! There's kerosene stored on the shelves, methylated spirit, everything would burst into flames, and we'd never get you out in time. You have to promise that you won't do anything so foolish. I'll tell Father . . .'

'It wouldn't make any difference, even if he moved me back upstairs. You can't watch me all night. If you don't get me the keys, that's what I'll do,' Frances said, ineffectually, for she knew that any fire lighting would be disastrous in that dry cellar with its shelves crammed with inflammable goods.

Helen recognized the idle threat for what it was, and picked up the tray. She moved slowly up the staircase, then hesitated and turned back. 'Frances,' she said. 'Would you do something for me? I know that I have no right to ask you. If they do send you to that place, if you see Paul there, would you please tell him that . . .'

'Tell him what?' Frances said harshly.

'Tell him that I feel so lonely. That I think about him all the time, every day. And that I still have the paper bird he made. He'll know what I mean. And that I ask, not ask, beg him to return to the temple. Even if he has to pretend, if he has to tell lies. It might not be too late. Perhaps the council would believe . . . at least we could still see each other . . .'

'I'll tell him,' Frances said. 'If he's still alive!'

'Helen,' Rosgrana called. 'Father says that you're not to stay down there talking to her.'

'If he's still alive,' Frances said viciously. 'You don't even know what happens to them in that place. If they've killed him, it will be your fault. You should have got out somehow and told the police, the day they sent him there. Some friend you are! He's probably dead, just like Claire's going to be. She'll die all right, if you don't help me get out and fetch proper help. But if he's still alive when I get sent to that place, I'll certainly give him your message. I'll tell him that you don't care about him at all! I'll say you think his life isn't worth anything. I'll tell him that you said he can die there for all you care. That's the message I'm going to give him, unless . . .'

Helen backed slowly up the stairs, and Frances gazed up into a face so sad, so filled with anguish that her voice faltered and broke. '. . . unless you get me those keys,' she whispered forlornly. She listened to the bolt sliding shut on the other side of the door. There was nothing else to do but go to bed.

The ceiling lamp shone directly into her eyes, its bulb encased in a wire cage. It seemed desperately symbolic of herself and all the Tyrell girls. She switched off the light, but the cellar was plunged into a darkness so tomblike that she quickly turned the light back on. She lay on the stretcher and stared up at the caged light, listening

194

to the house settle completely into its pattern of silence.

'All these weeks, and I never wrote my name anywhere,' she thought bleakly. 'The first place I missed out doing that. Now nobody will ever know I was here in this house.'

Nobody would know about her stay at the temple, either; nobody who mattered. 'It's not any better at the temple,' Helen had said. 'It's worse.' But in spite of thinking that, Helen chose to remain, going from one prison to the other.

Frances stopped listening hopefully for the sound of the door opening at the top of the stairs. It had been stupid of her to expect Helen to reverse the pattern of fifteen years. Helen's sole gesture towards freedom had been a pathetic little hole scratched in paint, made secretly in her room where nobody could discover it.

Frances thought of the times during those fifteen years when Helen could have possibly escaped from the house. Surely there must have been opportunities. 'She could have planned something with Paul,' Frances raged. 'The two of them could have worked something out. She's utterly useless, and it was a waste of time, asking her to help. She's just weak, weaker than anyone else in this house. Hanging up a stupid paper bird! Giving in for the sake of peace all the time . . . She's so scared, she'd watch her own sister die rather than do anything about it.'

She felt dizzy and sick with impotent anger.

When the rage was spent and replaced by over-whelming defeat, she lay like a stick of wood on the bed, gazing up at the light in its cage. Perhaps Helen was even right. It would be infinitely easier to give in, to submit your will to the temple; your life, even the small space behind your forehead where your private thoughts lay. At least that way you could gain some peace for yourself. What was the use of fighting, when you so obviously couldn't win? Helen was right, and she was in error. It had been pointless and even cruel to involve Helen.

'She'll forget about it in a couple of weeks, any-how,' Frances thought tiredly. 'She'll just go on as she's always done, pottering about in the garden and taking orders and just slipping away to her room when it all gets too hard to bear. I shouldn't have said that about Paul to her. It was spiteful, dragging it up. But she'll get over him, too, I expect, in a few weeks.'

Time dragged itself along as slowly and pain-fully as a wounded animal. She lost track of the hours, and when the little door at the top of the stairs was pushed open, she blundered out of her weariness, thinking that the whole night must have passed, and now they had come to take her away. She got to her feet stiffly and climbed the stairs, so that Mr Tyrell wouldn't have the satis-faction of coming down to fetch her by duress.

But it was Helen standing there, waiting. 'I stole the keys from his office,' she said dully. 'And I'll

196

have to go with you. I don't want to leave, but I can't stay, because he'd kill me for doing this. It's only because of Claire, because of Paul . . . I hate you for making me do this thing!' She turned away and set the key in the kitchen door, not looking at Frances at all. Frances watched, in an agony of slowly awakening cramped muscles. She listened to the muted, secret sounds of the house; a tap dripping, timbers stirring on the staircase, someone murmuring in their sleep. She imagined that the metallic turning of the key must be heard all over the house, right up to the little attic where Claire lay. Helen opened the door and the screen, which creaked sharply as she pushed against it. Terror rushed into her face, but Frances took her hand and led her gently out into the moonlit yard.

'We can't use the back gate,' Helen said. 'I don't know how to unlock the chain without setting the alarm off. We'll have to leave by the side gate and the front garden.'

Her hands trembled so badly that Frances took the key and unlocked the gate in the side wall. She eased it open, as softly as turning a page in a book, and gazed at the stretch of path beyond. It shone as white as ash in the moonlight, fringed by inky shadows, and the window of her aunt's and Mr Tyrell's room was half-way along its length. Frances could feel sweat crawling over her skin. She imagined Mr Tyrell watching from behind the curtain. Perhaps he had heard every sound of their leaving, listening in the cold winter silence.

Perhaps he was standing there now, biding his time like a cat at a mouse hole. Frances swallowed hard and set back her shoulders. She gripped Helen's hand and led her down the path as though it were a tightrope, past the dark eye of the window.

She took a deep breath and slowly opened the front gate. It swung stiffly on its hinges. Its lower edge scraped hideously across the cement path, shattering the silence of moonlight and shadow. Frances tugged at Helen's hand and ran. It was as though all the goblins and terrors of everyone's childhood were at her heels, lurched, grinning, in every shadow to pluck at her skirt as she sped by. She ran in irrational panic, and when Helen stumbled and fell, the terror plunged into cruelty. She used her nails to dig into flesh, kicked, abused Helen with all the ugly obscenities she knew. She hauled Helen to her feet without pity, and dragged her through endless empty streets, paying no heed to direction.

At the end of an immense distance, they stumbled onto a bridge, and on the far side of the bridge the city lay, glittering with lights under the sky. Frances collapsed against the parapet and listened to the wild racing of her heartbeat gradually regain its steady balance. No one had come after them. They were safe; alone and safe. She became aware of the sounds of weeping.

Helen was weeping softly into her cupped

hands, with an intense grief, so private and filled with lonely pain that Frances didn't intrude.

She stood quietly and watched the sleeping city, waiting for Helen to deal with her grief.

'I made her unlock the doors and end that sort of life for her family,' she thought. 'She's going to need help. All those years . . . I'll have to find someone who can tell her there's not going to be a war, and there's nothing to be scared of. I'll have to find Paul.'

She looked up at the winter sky, huge and wide and clean, brilliant with stars.

'She's never seen the stars properly, except through a tiny hole in a painted window,' Frances thought, waiting for Helen to finish her terrible grieving. 'When she stops crying, I'll show her the stars.'

About the author

Born in Kempsey, NSW, Robin Klein is one of nine children. Her great-grandfather was an Irish convict who was sentenced to life transportation to Australia for highway robbery.

Now a full-time writer, Robin Klein has worked at various jobs: tea lady, telephonist (got the sack for cutting people off at the switchboard), bookshop assistant (got into trouble for reading the books instead of selling them), library assistant, nurse, potter and copper enameller, and photography teacher.

She had her first short story published at the age of sixteen, and won her only school prize for writing. In 1981 she was awarded a Literature Board grant for writing, and has now had eight books published. In 1983 she won the Australian Junior Book of the Year award for *Thing*.

Robin Klein lives in a haunted cottage in the hills near Melbourne with one of her four children.